PRAISE FOR *THE LOST JOURNA[LS]*

AN INDIE NEXT PICK, SELECTE[D]

"A new version of the story of Sacajewea, centered on herself, her obstacles, her courage and her life." **—Minneapolis Star Tribune**

"Earling's Sacajawea rewrites the version of herself handed down through American history. Her life before the expedition comes into vivid focus, as do her complicated feelings about her role in charting the course for American imperialism." **—The Millions, Most Anticipated Books of 2023**

"Earling lets Sacajewea tell her own story, in her own voice, revealing a complex, determined woman who makes hard choices in the face of ongoing loss and violence. It's a beautiful and ultimately hopeful novel that lays bare many important truths about American history and myth-making." **—Book Riot, 20 Must-Read Indigenous Historical Fiction Books**

"The suffering—and bold, ingenious agency—of women held as captives by both Native and Euro-Americans is rendered with special vividness [. . .]. The narration is rich in realistic detail but animated by a dreamlike intensity [. . .]. Throughout the text, Sacajewea memorably enacts what Gerald Vizenor dubs survivance, the negotiation of existential challenges with a spirited, oppositional inventiveness. A profoundly moving imagining of the impressions and contributions of a major historical figure." **—Kirkus Reviews (starred)**

"At its surface, this may be a novel, but deeper down, it's a spirit-song, an invocation, a magical incantation. The language simultaneously keeps Sacajewea unknowable and gives us a path to greater understanding. The poetic prose elevates it from a tragic story to a founding mythic ethos of America. In this, Earling has given us a new model for the literature of the West. The *Lost Journals of Sacajewea* changes how novels will be written, or at least it should." **—Big Sky Journal**

"A FORMALLY INVENTIVE, HISTORICALLY EYE-OPENING NOVEL." —NEW YORK TIMES

"Offers new perspective on what is known, and debated, about the life of Sacajewea, including her age, her marriage to a French fur-trader (Toussaint Charbonneau), and her experience as the only woman traveling on the 1804–1806 Corp of Discovery expedition with Meriwether Lewis and William Clark. In poetic prose, Earling interweaves factual accounts of Sacajewea's life with a first-person narrative deeply rooted in the physicality of landscape and brutality of the times." **—Seattle Times**

"Earling adds a much-needed Native woman's perspective to Sacajewea's story, bringing a note of resilience to her unflinching account of the white men's violence and depredation: 'Women do not become their Enemy captors. We survive them.' This is a beautiful reclamation."
—Publishers Weekly

"The most remarkable thing about Debra Magpie Earling's second novel, *The Lost Journals of Sacajewea*, is how uncompromising it is in its vision of a precolonial consciousness. [. . .] Through Sacajewea's voice, Earling rejects traditional English narrative forms as well as the sanitized version of westward expansion. Sacajewea's words never delineate between her mind and her body, between people and the natural world around her, between the present and the eternal, between prose and poetry—dualities westerners and Western literature take for granted. As a result, the novel records a life story that at once feels representative of the historical violence Indigenous women have faced and survived, but also a life story burdened by a place in popular history that is not Sacajewea's, was never meant to be hers. [. . .] Earling gives fluidity in one's body, in one's place in society, in one's place in the natural world, that many Americans cannot fathom." **—Sewanee Review**

"[Earling's] lyrical novel brings this mythologized figure to life, casting unsparing light on the men who brutalized her and recentering Sacajewea as the arbiter of her own history, which is, ultimately, one of survival. [Earling's] book is a tool of and for empathy, not so much one of understanding each word or experience, but of feeling."**—Write Question**

More Praise for *The Lost Journals of Sacajewea*

"*The Lost Journals of Sacajewea* is a wonder! Earling reclaims Sacajewea from non-Native histories and characterizations and restores the fulness of her being. She unflinchingly depicts the complexities of a girl navigating layers of trauma, yet preserves Sacajewea's agency and power. Earling's Sacajewea tells us a new story, closer to the bone. In gorgeous, startling, revelatory prose, the author commands the English language in profound ways, shapes it to her purposes, and designs a new speech. *The Lost Journals of Sacajewea* is a literary masterpiece, a whirlwind of a story that made me shiver in response to its difficult beauty."
—**Susan Power, author of** *Sacred Wilderness*

"*The Lost Journals of Sacajewea* is an immensely moving and transcendental work of literature. Debra Magpie Earling masterfully tells a story with prose so determined and so full of light and beauty that it's impossible to look away. This is a striking, elegant, and impressive work of art that persists in the reader's mind even after the book has ended."
—**Morgan Talty, author of** *Night of the Living Rez*

"*The Lost Journals of Sacajewea* is a masterpiece, not just of historical fiction, but of any genre. This raw and bracing retelling of Sacajewea's life is a thorough dismantling of the legend of the Corps of Discovery, to be sure. But in line after stunning line, Earling reveals Sacajewea in an astonishing and heartbreaking fulness. This sublime book will leave you shook and touched at once, on every single page."
—**Smith Henderson, author of** *Make Them Cry*

"Debra Magpie Earling's gorgeous retelling of Sacajewea's journey shatters modern-day narrative conventions and documented history. With mesmerizing language and incantatory rhythms, Earling delivers an urgent accounting from the *true world* in a work that feels more alive

than written. Yes, alive in a way I didn't recognize—yet still felt! How deeply, deeply I fell into this story. The bottom line is that *The Lost Journals of Sacajewea* is an awakening, a revelation, a devastating triumph, and a literary magic act."
—**Adrianne Harun, author of** *A Man Came Out of a Door in the Mountain*

"If the Olympics awarded medals for feats of the imagination, this book would be good for the Gold. Marvelously dreamed, starkly and poetically told. The story of the Lewis and Clark Expedition will never be the same."
—**Ted Kooser, author of** *Delights & Shadows*

"Not since James Welch's monumental *Fools Crow* has such an immersive work of narrative genius risen out of the West. In luminous, image-laden prose, as if by way of elemental reconstitution, Debra Magpie Earling awakens a voice that our American mythology had hoped would stay sleeping, and in so doing unearths *The Lost Journals of Sacajewea*, a harrowing—though ultimately triumphant—once-in-a-generation work of art."
—**Chris Dombrowski, author of** *The River You Touch*

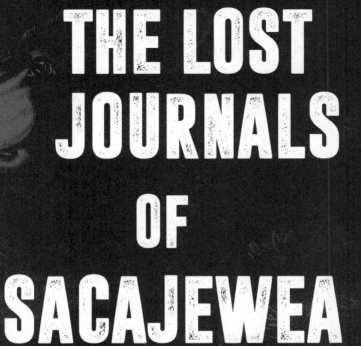

THE LOST
JOURNALS
OF
SACAJEWEA

ALSO BY DEBRA MAGPIE EARLING

Perma Red

THE LOST JOURNALS
OF
SACAJEWEA

a novel

DEBRA MAGPIE EARLING

MILKWEED EDITIONS

First paperback edition, published 2024 by Milkweed Editions
Printed in Canada
Cover design by Mary Austin Speaker
Cover art by John James Audubon
24 25 26 27 28 5 4 3 2 1

978-1-63955-074-6

Library of Congress Cataloging-in-Publication Data

Names: Earling, Debra Magpie, author.
Title: The lost journals of Sacajewea / Debra Magpie Earling.
Description: First edition. | Minneapolis, Minnesota : Milkweed Editions,
    2022. | Summary: "From the award-winning author of Perma Red comes a
    devastatingly beautiful novel that challenges prevailing historical
    narratives of Sacajewea"-- Provided by publisher.
Identifiers: LCCN 2022038367 (print) | LCCN 2022038368 (ebook) | ISBN
    9781571311450 (hardcover) | ISBN 9781571317742 (epub)
Subjects: LCSH: Sacagawea--Fiction. | LCGFT: Biographical fiction. |
    Novels.
Classification: LCC PS3605.A765 L68 2022 (print) | LCC PS3605.A765
    (ebook) | DDC 813/.6--dc23/eng/20221004
LC record available at https://lccn.loc.gov/2022038367
LC ebook record available at https://lccn.loc.gov/2022038368

Milkweed Editions is committed to ecological stewardship. We strive to align our book
production practices with this principle, and to reduce the impact of our operations in
the environment. We are a member of the Green Press Initiative, a nonprofit coalition
of publishers, manufacturers, and authors working to protect the world's endangered
forests and conserve natural resources. *The Lost Journals of Sacajewea* was printed on
acid-free 100% postconsumer-waste paper by Friesens Corporation.

For the stolen sisters of all Native Nations

Dear Reader,

My elders say not long ago we were able to blend into our environment the way animals do. Like bears we could step into the brush and vanish from sight. The ability arose from something deep within us, blood instinct and survival, the oldest kind of knowledge. When guns and horses gave advantage over our enemies, we no longer needed innate camouflage. The more interaction we had with the unnatural world, the less we relied on our instinctual abilities.

In *The Lost Journals of Sacajewea*, communication is Sacajewea's hold on the instinctual. Language is her digging stick to memory, her song, her tap-tapping into old knowledge in order to survive. Sounds are alive to her. Instead of ellipses I use two or more successive periods— . . —to indicate pauses. These periods are her heart and drum beats.

The double periods— . . —also suggest stuttered awe when she witnesses events that are inviolable.

She believes that written and spoken words can manifest the "thing" itself. For that reason, sacred names, ideas, or words that should not be uttered are italicized and appear faded.

When people are significant or require negotiation and/or deference, names are capitalized. Sacajewea determines the hierarchal relationship to the people and animals around her.

History has long been translated by the powerful, so Sacajewea's translations and transfigurations become her power. She captures the living breath through sound. Nouns become verbs. Verbs become vibrations. Punctuation echoes natural pauses. People are re-remembered through the lens of trauma and loss.

On the precipice of colonization she finds emancipation through her own peculiar language. Lines are shattered to reveal spiritual expansiveness.

The woman known as Sacajawea by the Lemhi Shoshone appears only a handful of times in the voluminous journals of Lewis and Clark. Her name—and later her tribal identity—her marriage, her age, the date of her death, even her role in the expedition as interpreter, guide, or friendly talisman to ward off hostile tribes is fraught. An enslaved young girl traveling with a military expedition spoils the long held notion that the expedition was wholesome.

And yet, two hundred years after the Lewis and Clark Expedition the "historical" Sacajawea codifies an account that does not sully the discovery narrative. She does not speak. She does not fight back in visible ways. She participates. Or does she?

The Lost Journals of Sacajewea is a fictional account of the life of Sacajawea. Her story, like all human stories, is sacrosanct, but her story remains an undeniable testament to the power of cultural knowledge and resistance. Sacajawea survived what many could not.

DME
November 28, 2022

"Darkness doesn't kill the light—it defines it."

—Richard Wagamese

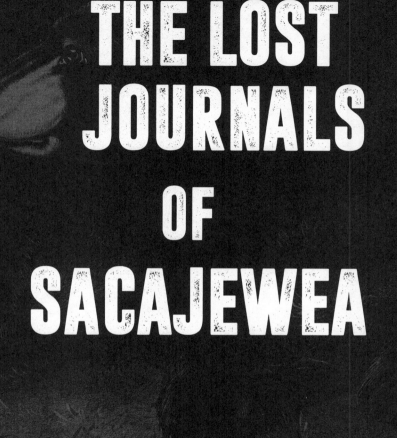

THE LOST
JOURNALS
OF
SACAJEWEA

DAYS
OF AGAI

In my seventh winter, when my head only reached my Appe's rib, a White Man came into camp. Bare trees scratched Sky. Cold was endless. He moved through trees like strikes of Sunlight. My Bia said He came with bad intentions like a Water Baby's cry.

Old Ones said this Man was the craziest White Man they had seen. Young Ones said this was the only White Man they had seen. Our wise One, Flatbird, asked Agai River if this was the very White Man sent from our Old Stories, but River did not answer.

See. He does not come with Horses, People said. He does not have pelts to trade.

In that black winter, His clothes were tattered, brittle-cold; they fell from Him in pieces like leaves fall from Trees. Snow had scraped His feet to bones.

At first, People were afraid of Him. How did He survive? People asked. Only a crazy One could survive with no covering and no food.

He is no Man, some said. Look at His skin.

His skin was frail pond ice when Moon lifts day. He shook like a dog shakes water. Crazy shaking. Day and night He shook. My Appe fed Him and covered Him with our best robes.

For many days, White Man sat beside our cook fire rubbing His palms together. He was like a hunk of frozen Buffalo; He stole the fire heat. And after many days, He became like the white Trees that line the Turtle marsh. His bark peeled. We saw bone shine, His back bared to wings. His fingers thawed, slushed, then stank. His penis turned to ash.

Our People came to look before He died. Touched His head. Prayed.

Flatbird said, I have no Medicine for this crazy Man. His eyes are washed of color.

See. He is already turning to Sky.

I sat with the dying Man. I watched over Him, as my Appe asked. White Man lived to see tall grass return, lived to welcome Agai—Agai so thick in River we heard them speak. White Man lived to see us dance and watched us with His lowered head like an Elk with swivel eyes.

White Man lived to fool us.

He lived.

Follow Him, my Appe told me. Learn His tongue. Find out what He knows.

My Bia did not like White Man. She chewed Deer hides soft, made many baskets, all the while her scout eye perched on me, on Him, on His hands' pale flutter around everything I touched, and did.

This Man spoke a strange tongue. All day long He spoke. On and on He spoke. His words made no sense.

What do you think He is saying? my Appe asked. He is all the time talking.

Fa Ra Siss Huck Ja Ja Ta To Eat Pa Ra, I said.

Appe took me to River to fish. Alone. He hid me from Bia.

I will teach you to fish, Appe said, so that you will know. Far off you will know to fish to stay alive. You must know how to speak to Water, but it is All to know how to listen. Listen like River listens to Agai.

When we netted enough to feast, Appe prayed. For a long time, he prayed. And then Appe struck River bushes with two sticks. He tossed head-sized rocks into tall grasses and grass Birds beat their wings like drums and flapped around us and away.

Appe cupped his ears. He looked to see if White Man followed me, if Bia was near. From all signs we were alone. He took off his moccasins and signaled me to follow. He took hold of my hand and together we stepped into the strong current of Debai-lit

Water. We hid deep in shadowy scratch where bramble roots become one with River. Water was cold. Agai trembled close to our feet and held to us. I crouched beside Appe in hiss-speak of Water. I listened. I watched.

Appe looked down into Water and hooped his arms. Currents cracked over smooth stones and shivered around us. He waited until a round seam of Water appeared. Waves rushed past his circled arms. He waited until his breath no longer puffed.

Appe pulled me into the center of River, a still circle. I hold you here, my Baide. I ask River keep you as safe as I do now. As long as you are near River Water, I send my spine, my string gut, my blood to protect you.

I had a trouble dream, my Baide, Appe told me. In my dream, my own Baide spoke many tongues. Water chose her to be *Long Spirit* who remains after all are no more. A strong Baide who must speak with Monsters.

I was Appe's only Baide. He was speaking about me, but did not wish his dream to fall over me.

I peered down into the clear River spot, but saw only Agai, their long snouts, their red fins flutter, their round round eyes.

Our Old Ways protect you, he said. Give me your hand. Can you feel it, Baide? River shakes tiny shakes now. *No-longer-living* is here. Feel it in your gut, my Baide. Earth changing, moving away from us. Little by little it goes.

Do not let Monsters know you understand. Hold to yourself and you will be safe, Appe said.

I opened my hands and held them over River and felt shaking in me. Outside me.

Sickness is near, Appe said.

We heard People of Sagebrush were struck by sudden Sickness. Black circles boiled up from deep in their bodies, burst, and robed them in antler velvet. The People died like rotten plums, split open, their skin fizzing stink. Their faces turned the color of Mountains before dark. Whole Villages rotted. Their angry *Spirits* plague Rivers now. Villages of *Spirits* searching for what was taken.

Appe knew what others did not know. Not Flatbird. Not Bia. Not Cameahwait.

Can you hear Them? Appe asked. Trees scream with wind at night. Fury spits from Debai-lit skies and breaks branches in darkened woods. Their anger rattles rocks along River edge. Seething. Chittering. Close and All Around. So many lost. The Sickness they carry jickles like dry seedpods. Like Bad Medicine crouches in bone. Soon we will all be touched by Sickness we cannot heal.

Listen to me Baide. One day you will be far from me. But what we have taught will not leave you. Learn all you can and you will go on. From here now, and for many generations, far far into where I cannot see—you will be. I cannot tell you how, he said.

My Appe's words trembled in me. All day my knees shook.

White Man looked at clouds. Slept like a baby in a bundle cradle.

Bia and I gathered Tree nuts, brown grass seeds. You look like trouble coming, Bia said to me. You are too young to be broken-mouthed. Your face is tatter-poled as an old Woman teepee carrier.

It is the wind, all night, I said.

Puh, Bia said. It is you drag White Man around like pull dog. I see. I see it is no good for you.

Listen. Learn from Him, Appe told me when we were alone.

How come Bia does not wish me to learn from White Man? I asked.

I think you ask why she does not believe me. Appe laughed. No People live long without One-Who-Challenges. We fall asleep in our tasks. Your Bia is like the dog that yaps at Weta. Weta growls and sniffs and digs with big claws. But Bia keeps her push. She is not afraid of sharp teeth or Weta snarls. Maybe she is right. You decide.

Bia saw what Appe did not see and Appe saw what Bia did not see.

You must hear the White Man's voice, Baide, Bia said. You must hear Him differently than our Men hear. We Women hold our People's language, and our language. Your own language is here, she said. She patted my chest.

Bia held my face and whispered, Men do not know Woman carries a voice inside her to help her live. When you stop hearing your voice you are nothing more than snare bait. You are bone crackles in Weta's teeth.

Bia and Appe followed me. Buzzed around me.

Listen, Appe said. Listen to the steady tap of bees as they butt their tails against flowers.

Listen, Bia said, to the heavy smack of Wetas' tongues against their teeth.

Listen, Appe said, to wind as it catches in Land dips.

Listen, Bia said, to the slather-drool in a hungry Wolf's mouth. And in a Man's mouth, she said. Puh.

Bia listened with the backs of her hands and the back of her head. She listened with her rumble gut.

All things have their own way of being in this World, Bia said, a pattern, a footprint, sounds to make babies laugh, sounds to make children see trouble. Hear this, my Baide, in the gristle chew around campfires, in the laughter and mean jokes All Around, listen close. Stay awake. All speak carries warning—the tight-foot tread of Coyote around camp Water, the yowl of Fox throwing his voice, the scary titter of Agai when Water bowls in shallows. Listen to the White Man to survive. Let his voice set up in your head like coagulated blood along the ridges of scalps.

I listened as I made moccasins for White Man. I listened as I made Him Deer shirt and leggings. He wobbled like a fawn behind me. He talked and talked. He talked every bush, every blossom, every seed. I came to understand my own voice through His voice. Every tongue tap. Every voice Song. And then, slowly, White Man's sounds became words and His words held meaning.

This I learned from Him: He came from Civilization.

His people came from across
big Water.

His Medicine *Spirit* was Jesus +

He had seen the Devil.

His people have many many words
for the World.

He tried to teach me all of them.

When White Man could not walk far He used me as His walking stick. He gripped my shoulders and stumbled behind me. Bia slapped His hands if He fell me. She stayed as close to Him as a suck bug. He watched me as I picked berries, plucked grasses, kept cook fires, dried Agai, played games.

You work as hard as a Man, He told me. But you are a little girl.

I did not understand and He pointed to young Men and cradled His cheek in His hand and closed His eyes. He put His arms around a large rock, grunted, and pointed at me. He smiled.

I looked away. He smiled too much. He smiled at everything like He knew something we did not know. He could not know our ways. The way Men work. The way Women work. Women hands are stained with blood, childbirth, and Men's blood. Ripe berries. Butcher blood. He could not know I work harder than Men because I am learning All Ways to survive.

Women carry childbirth and Death, blister snow and suckling babies, Weta growls and Weta attacks in berry bushes, Enemy sneak-ups, War parties return, and War parties not return. Women survive carry-work every day. All year. Year upon year. Across Prairies. Across Rivers. Across Mountains. In All Ways, Women carry Men in all their ways. Women carry Men to survive.

White Man was as lazy as a lazy Bird plucking lice from a Horse butt.

Appe told me to keep listening.

White Man drew scratches in soft River edges. This line means the beginning of a word. This is the word for SUN. He lifted His hand to Debai and drew a circle with spikes and pointed to His scratching, then pointed up to Debai. The round white circle in the Sky, SUN, He said.

When Weta snuffled in the willows, He pointed. Bear, He said. Dangerous Bear. He made his hands curl like Weta claws and clawed Sky. He named all the Fish. He named Everything.

There are four Seasons, He said. Winter brings cold and snow. The opposite of Winter is Summer. Summer brings heat, days of plenty. Spring brings renewal, new leaves, new hope, new Life. Autumn brings frost and shimmers with golden leaves. He lifted his palm toward River and pulled his fingers together as if He sprinkled fat over soup. Shimmer, He said. Glitter. His eyes watered. Light over Water is beautiful. Autumn is beautiful, He said.

You are beautiful, He said.

When I asked what beautiful means, He swept his open hand across the Landsight from Earth to Sky to Earth.

Beautiful, He said. He touched small red-speckled leaves. Beautiful, He said again, lifting tiny rosebuds to my face. Beautiful.

Puh, Beautiful means He has come to destroy us, Bia said. He is foolish. Pay no attention to His petting words. Only what He does. Petting words will fool you. What He does is what matters. Remember our long-ago stories. He is only one of many Enemies to come.

I listened to Bia and tried to understand the many ways she told me to listen and not listen. I became as watchful as Coyote blinking in the underbrush.

White Man ways of living are strange to our ways. If all White Men live in blind Seasons, they are like a Man with one foot snared. They are asleep to the changing Moons. I was born in the Season of Budding Moon. Bia said I was born to understand plants and to use them to their best. I was born to gather, to see the World around me, to listen, to tend. Appe was born in the Season of Coyote Moon. He was born to track, to watch, to pay attention. He sees things we cannot. Bia was born in the Season of Rutting Moon. No one has to be told this. It is clear she is always toothed with anger, bubbling steam, loud. No body, no animal, no change gets in her way. I did not ask White Man what Season He was born in or what His name was. He told me He wished to live free from the Life He once lived. Free from the People He once knew.

When White Man spotted Pop Pank swimming, He dove under River ice to grab her and she dipped her head, and disappeared. He dove down, again and again. He dove into River where only *Water Spirits* go. He tried until His belly turned blue and His white skin shook like a blanket of mice. He rose empty-handed every try.

He held my shoulders, and Bia looked up from her cook fire. Crows flapped, clawed smoke, grasped and flittered and squawked away.

I heard of your People's Medicine, White Man said. But I have never witnessed it before now. His eyes were bluster blue. His eyes were ruptured eyes spilling blue beads. He clapped. His spittle silver beads. If I could have plucked His eyes, I would have made a necklace. His eyes were beautiful. I would have sewn His eyes on to my robe.

Pop Pank is not like ordinary People, He said. Do you understand? White Man was Crow at first feeding. Crow laughing at a broken gut spilling maggots. *ă'-rah*

Ordinary, He said again. Like you and me. He pointed to me and then to Himself.

He squatted low and then pointed to Pop Pank wrapped in a blanket beside her Gagu, Mud Squatter.

Pop Pank has what my People call magic, He said. He made a fist and opened His fingers to Sky. She can do the impossible. She can breathe underwater. White Man made the sign for Fish and then pointed again to Pop Pank. He shook His head and smiled like an old Man who returns from battle with more scalps than wounds. He looked at Pop Pank like a baby looks at what-cannot-be-seen.

What did He see? Pop Pank was a runt among runts. She had lived through five turns of Seasons. Her knees were knobbly as Moose legs. Her hair did not grow. She could run as fast as any Woman, and faster than any Man, but she had a thin, broken look. She did not work like Women worked. She learned her ways from her Gagu. All day they swam together through Seasons. I looked and looked until I saw what He saw.

Pop Pank was sinew and bone, small as a Trout. Her eyes were the color of marsh Water—murky, muddy, and come together like a teardrop at the center. Fish eyes.

She is different, White Man said. She is special among all others.

I learned Pop Pank would be special among White People. I learned White Man was no longer related to animals.

When seed grasses rattled and second summer came blue-Mooned and hazy, White Man wrapped Himself in grass blankets I taught Him to weave. He took Appe's Horse and rode into the Trees where He had come from. He rode away at first rising when mice skitter beneath dry grass shells and Buffalo flowers lift their heads.

Puh, Bia said to gathered Women. He was no good. I told you. I told all of you. We should have killed Him when He was pitiful. Now He steals our Horse and laughs. He was not crazy. Puh. He was all along Enemy. He was all along worthless thief.

White Man promised He would come back. I waited for Him. I stood beside River and listened. I stepped into knee-deep Water where slippery roots catch ankles to hear the Faraway. I dreamt of Agai crying, breaking their long bodies on rocks as they leapt up and over Water falls and Ogres, to return *Long Spirit* to us. I watched the edge-of-dark-woods where He had first shown His self and Bia grabbed me and told me to be awake to what was.

White Man will return, Bia said. There will be no good Medicine in His comeback. He will curse us with His many Brothers. He will return like lice.

I did not see White Man again.

Flatbird said, this White Man was *bad Spirit* come to tell what is to come. All Around us, Flatbird said, All Around.

Puh, Bia whispered. What do I not know?

GATHER DAYS AT THREE FORKS

Day of Moon turning to ash

We are camped by Three Rivers Come Together—out on the wide grasses far from Agai. I am nine winters aged. In my gut, Land tells me we are not wanted in this place of Earth mounds and distant Mountains, growl-thick with Moose stink, marshy suck holes, and sneaky boat-headed Badgers.

Last Gather Season, our Enemy the Apsáalooke, killed our Walk-Around-Watchers. They ran us from our gathering places before Buffalo came, before we cached what keeps us. Some winters come like Rabbits, soft-round with snowy robes. Some winters slip down Mountains like scat, like gut-stench steam, winters that punish us with reek Waters and boney Wolves.

Starvation winter came like bitter smoke from screech-dry Rivers. Our mouths turned blue with hunger. Winter itself—a hungry animal—snuffled on the high ridges, roared down Mountainsides, howled ice-cuts across wide-open. Trees snapped around us. Agai River whined. Our skinny Horses ate sticks and grew barrel-stomached.

Now we have so much meat I feel stingy with all Earth gives.

I pray all day as I work but tire of work all day.

Women work day into night.

Men clatter down Mountains with more Deer. More Elk, sometimes Antelope, and living thud-jumpy Rabbits. As I skin, I dream of gathering Camas roots and Gooseberries.

Animals give their lives to our hunger. I thank them as I skin. I use every speck. My fingernails are red-Mooned and blood smell. After Ceremony, I skin Deer, skin Antelopes, skin Weasels, skin Buffalo, skin Rabbits, skin Elk. My blood-heavy robe sticks to my belly. Blood-gut days. My teeth ache with beating and breaking bones. Scraping hides. Nothing is left but stacks of shatter bones to grind.

When Moon rises work saws in my teeth. Scrape scrape scrape. You should work clean, Men tell me.

You should be happy, my Bia says. We won't starve come winter.

Bia works beside me, her back a Hunter's bow. We have shattered so many backbones, have pounded bone on bone for one slurp of marrow. My hands are as wide as my Appe's. My knuckle cracks wake mice.

Appe is the person all Hunters seek. He is arrow fixer and arrow maker. His bows are as bendable and as strong as Agai. His bows do not shoot arrows; his bows spin arrows to their aim. No Hunter misses with an arrow made from Appe. He fixes thick arrows or bent arrows, and whittles them down so they sing through Sky. His bows, covered with snake skins, are never lost. Appe's snake-skinned bows writhe. Appe makes nets that capture more Agai than ten Men with large nets. His fishing spears chant through roaring Waters and spear mightiest Agai. His arrows whisper to the hearts of Deer and Elk. Hunters repay Appe with plenty meat.

At Three Rivers Come Together, heavy sacks of meat swing over us, dripping blood. Black and flapping Birds darken Sky.

White Man called ă'-rah Crow. Now ă'-rah and Crow are one in my head.

Their name ă'-rah like their call. Their name Crow like they look.

Crows rootle lice, shit on the blackened Tree stand, and scold Women working

ă'-rah

ă'-rah

ă'-rah   ă'-rah

until Debai sleeps.

I am small and Crows wing down to snatch entrails from my hands. Crows are a shining black lake of wings above, around me.

Women look up from work and laugh when they hear me scream. They will take you, they tell me. We will see the speck of you in the Sky   far   far   from us.

Black beads of ă'-rah. Crow eyes surround me, follow me. Crow eyes like small pecking winds of Old Women eyes. Like Old Women who know—me, you, All Around. Crows bobble over stacks of bones pecking blood, their eyes watching All Ways.

ă'-rah

Crows know my prayers are puny. They know I want to go home to Agai. They know my want means we suffer from hunger the length of long winter. They laugh at me. *ă'-rah ha ha*

At night the amber-green glow of Mountain Cats surround our camp, their eyes glaring in the Trees. So much blood makes us all prey.

Day of Moppo

When Debai rolls behind Mountains, clouds lift from oily reeds. Mists rise from nests of mud. Blood-stinger s s swirl. Blood-stingers s s swell.

Moppo.

Water bush pitch and Sweetgrass burn all night. Smoke to chase Moppo back.

Too Ott Lok, pitiful one, cannot outrun Moppo, cannot hide. They find him. They seek him out.

Old Men say, Stay far from Too Ott Lok. Watch for him. He is not like other boys.

We hear high sing hum-m of him-m long before we see him. At dusk, night Birds whistle-roar around him. Open-throat Bats whoop the Sky, descend like Appe's arrows to spear Too Ott Lok clouds. Birds clear mists swarming Too Ott Lok's head. Bats and Birds swoop his-s sweet blood.

We do not want him near our foot games. Children run from him and look back. Too Ott Lok, we call. Sticky gum catcher. Your blood is pine pitch and bee spit. Stay clear. Step back. Too Ott Lok comes.

Puh, Bia says. Too Ott Lok is our great gift. See. He was born to keep pests from us.

Bia is All Big when we are with Women. They listen to her words while she puffs and shudders.

Poor poor Too Ott Lok, Bia says. We should be happy he is with us.

Women look toward Bia with drum-stretch smiles. Nod like dogs catching scraps.

When we are alone, Bia tells me, Do not treat your own like always-baby. Better to leave one like him where you squat.

Days of no-work thief

Combs Gut does not leave Too Ott Lok who is thirteen winters old. She lugs him with us—everywhere, her baby, her big afterbirth saddle.

Rancid pair. Worse than rot, Otter Woman says. Combs Gut only works for Too Ott Lok. No one else.

Old Women strapped with baskets and burden-strap shoulders pretend Too Ott Lok is not sneaking behind them, scooping handfuls of berries—fistfuls—wolfing their work.

Too Ott Lok and Combs Gut, puh. Bia says their names like they are mice in her basket. Puh.

Too Ott Lok makes Gather Season long. Some nights, Combs Gut sings to him. If we listen, we hear her cooing without end. Most days, she stands behind him and rocks him in her arms, and together they pockell us as we pick chokecherries and gather high black moss.

He needs me, Combs Gut cries. We all must help him.

No one argues. Women always work .. always catch up slow Men.

When Women are not looking, Otter Woman and I spit plum stones at Too Ott Lok.

Toothless Onion Wife gums her tongue, looks at the ground. Her silence winks in the mouths of other Women.

Combs Gut eats more meat than Warriors but is only rib skin. Year upon year upon year she has not birthed children, still her teats bloat with milk. She binds her teats with tongue leaves wound with gut string. When her teats leak she cradles them in Cattails, and her teats leak .. .. and leak .. ..

How come she carries milk? I ask.

These things are not to be talked, my Bia says. Look with your gut, Baide then you would have no need for questions. Do not let your eyes hunt for no good. Puh.

Bia claps her palms over my eyes and shakes my head. You are here to work. Not weigh.

No one tells Too Ott Lok to work. He is many summers beyond me and still not a Man. He will not be. Too Ott Lok is Women-whispers, old Men long-looks, Children-laughs.

Bia pats my back and looks off into far away. She has taught me Old Ways to survive. She tells me Women carry Water pick berries dry berries collect help plants dig roots dig potatoes gather firewood snare game gut Deer gut Antelope gut Buffalo gut Weta pound meat pound meat & berries pound bones sew robes pound more meat seek mouse beans smoke hides weave Fish catches twist Agai nets pick berries pound berries dry berries dry roots pound roots dry Agai dry meat pound Fish smoke Fish smoke meat store cache gather Lodge poles put up Lodges sweep Lodges brush Horses tan hides cook tend fires weave grass braid grass cut willows scrape willow sticks weave willow baskets chew hides scrape roots scrape hides gather black Tree moss dig cooking holes cut bushes weave baskets tool root diggers snare lizards skin Porcupines make Porcupine brushes teeth quills wash roots find poison boil roots gather plums gather cherries grind bones gather clay burn cooking rocks gather cooking rocks make dog-carry carry cooking rocks carry children carry old ones carry firewood carry Water carry meat carry sacks carry Lodge poles carry carry carry.

When I fall asleep Bia is still talking. *Strike stones for tools make awls weave Agai gigs make bone caches make Sheep cups make Buffalo cups dry Deer brains boil Deer brains clean hides in Water wring hides wring hides wring hides make frames make drying pouch for frames make sinew ties chew sinew ties roll hides in ashes then smolder fires ..*

Before Debai enters our Lodge, Bia talks. Women make Earth jars. Fish kettles. Women hunt. Join War parties. She says more but my listening grows lazy.

No easy work, she tells me, only good work. See. All good work. All. Look at brush berries growing ripe to feed others. Look at Rabbits with their babies. Weta dig their food. Birds make nests, sit on eggs, chase us when we come close. Fox carries their babies to safety. Black moss grows as long as hair to feed us.

Too Ott Lok carries nothing but his fat self, I say.

I know work. I could speak my days, but talk is lazy.

I am not lazy. I work. More.

Bia whispers in my ear with breathed wings of Bats. We should leave him. Puh.

Bia's thoughts scrape like sharp bone. Her thoughts belong to many Women. What-Women-will-not-say calls in me. They say *Leave him. Leave him. Leave him. And go. Leave him and do not look back.*

It is not meanness, Appe says to me. It is survival.

It is meanness, Bia says. Puh. Meanness for survival.

Days before Thunder

On good days, Onion Wife tells Running Woman stories. Every Woman stops digging, stops picking, stops rooting to hear Onion Wife. Running Woman could hunt. Could trap. Could fight. Could weave grass baskets. Men, Women, Children watched Her like She was Debai, like She was Bluebird's light in dark Trees, like She was cold Water on a hot day. We watched Her sick with want for Her. She was smells of cook fires and Stream Waters, small Trees high in Mountains. Her skin glistened like Fox fur. Her teeth were strong as Elk teeth, white as River clay.

One cold night when the People were hungry, She returned from Far away—Her Horse weighted with Buffalo, Her dog-sled heavy with Antelope and Deer. We danced. We ate. No Man, no Woman was jealous of Her.

She left us in the Season of Thunder. Kidnapped by the River Lodge People and taken far from us. Our Men chased after the takers and returned sick and skinny. We knew She would escape these Enemies. For many days, we cried and waited. We looked for Her. We searched for Her. Every wind carried Her scent. Every Coyote sniff was Her breath. Every Mountain Lion cry was Her calling for us. For a long while People said they would see Her, a Lightening shot there, and then gone. Others swore they saw Her by River weaving rushes. We looked to find Her shadow cast like River shine through high ridge Trees. It has been a long time. We wait for Her until there is no One to wait.

Onion Wife claps her hands. You will see. Running Woman will return with drifts of Buffalo robes and pale pink shells. It will be like She was never gone.

You must gather what you can now. Fill your baskets to the top. When Running Woman returns, She will not find us lazy.

Night of too-good-for-you husband

My Bia has spoken.

Long ago, Appe promised me to Blue Elk. I am told when I am older, Blue Elk will take me for his first wife. This is my Appe's way of tricking, I think. If other Men believe Blue Elk wants me—they might want me.

Now old Women sigh. Young Women snort when they near me.

Blue Elk is <u>all</u> Women desire. They chase him, bring him hump fat of Buffalo, bull berries, Water potatoes, wet chewed hides, Water baskets. Every Bia wants to snatch Blue Elk for a monappe. With Blue Elk you will never go hungry, never worry about Enemies.

Women whisper Blue Elk is more. I watch them watch him.

When Debai pools red and night turns the blue shine of his hair. When mint and sting weed rile me like black poison arrow tips fallen to sharp grass, and Men watch for rainbowed Trout to stub against weirs, Blue Elk crouches in fields, gathers sage and needle grasses, and then rubs a fire that burns like lit Buffalo bellies, yellow in the vein-colored dark. Women watch as Blue Elk, sure as Fox, winds to Water, his torch light blazing above him flicking tiny Stars into night's bowl, All Around him tiny Stars raining, never catching brush on fire.

Men waiting for Fish run, open their mouths at the sight. Blue Elk lifts his torch and Fish gather to him, flapping Water. He gives his torch to Stands Tooth. He scoops up Fish and tosses them onto the bank, over and over again, until Blue Elk himself becomes one with Fishes. Blue Elk, his hair to his waist, belly flat, turns from Water to bank with armloads of Moon-speckled Fishes. His Song lifts like cedar smoke, like Womb ache. Silver curves of Rainbow Fish dance around him.

To be one with him would make Turtles sing, Women say.

Puh. How he looks matters less than mouse turds, Bia says. Who cares if his hair shines like Moon light? Who cares if his poker is as big as a Lodge pole?

Foolish Women. Foolish girls, Bia says. Do you not know arrows glance off his chest as if they know him? When no Deer are to be found, he finds them.

Bia speaks as loud as River roar. His looks will become as dry as old creek mud. Puh. Your belly will never rumble with Blue Elk in your Lodge.

But Women only gawp, only chitter chitter chitter like branch rub.

Day of blood sign

Small Elk left his Bia's side while she picked berries. Our whole camp made a game circle and we flushed toward each other, beating the ground with branches, closing in on ourselves.

Deer rattled bushes in the center of our search. Badger sniffed air and then clawed back into his hole. Weta and her two cubs shot past us shitting berries.

We should have gathered up and left before we lost Small Elk, I tell Bia.

Now a bad scent follows us. Death rattles in the leaves and tickle grass.

Women arch their backs and hiss as they enter River.

We are in the Season where Women blood scent is sticky. Old Women snuckle their gums, and say—Women-blood fouls Water.

Bia says, Women blood scent is winter calling us to prepare. See, Bia says, Bramble is as red as Womb. I will help you prepare, my Baide.

I am not ready to be Woman. Women-blood is strong enough to kill Men. Women-blood curdles Agai runs, rusts stones, salt clay, Elk trails, Turtle shells, Earth cracks. Women spill birth blood, and walk. Women-blood drums to all living. Our blood is our Song into Seasons.

My breasts are flat. My muscles flinch when I move. I am as muscly as a paw cat and far
from my blood time. I am not ready to lie beside Blue Elk, to open to him.

You will, my Baide, Bia says.

I will be like Running Woman, I say.

Bia laughs. She laughs so hard she spits. You have a slow start, she says.

We shut our eyes before we dunk beneath pull currents, afraid we will see edges-of-dark.

Bia hears Pabihiano hissing from River's edge, laughing, playing tricks. Can you not hear them? Pabihiano wait to net us in the Season before Turtle sleep, she whispers.

I do not tell her I hear Pabihiano when I am alone. They call to me. They rustle in River Tree overhangs. They tell me when I am too close to suck holes.

In Gather Season rough as gopher fields, Ogres chatter in River foam but only Appe sees.

They have left their stone houses and bunched up here, Appe says. He sniffs. Up River is clogged with Sickness and bones of the Dead. Do not look.

I shiver when I enter Water. I watch for change.

Days of Earth yawn

After Rutting Season the days are hot as summer stones and promise sweet roots and plenty Deer, but just below River skin, Death pulls. Rattlers shed their long skins along hilly rocks and fury-strike any move. Lightning crawls Earth like lizards, shivers over gather paths, and the paths of all animals. Thunder rumbles our feet and startles blood.

Now is the time young Women see only each other, and only as Enemy. They hear their own Womb rattle and ready themselves to strike.

Move out of their way, old Women tell young Men, and laugh. For young Women, there is only one Enemy now—Bawitčhuwa.

Women eye Bawitčhuwa. They watch Her like camp scouts and stretch their eyeballs to keep Her in sight. If Bawitčhuwa spots them, they play blind. They play they look to distant Mountains.

Bawitčhuwa is fourteen winters and ready for Husband. She is as ripe as late Season snow berries, and poison.

Even old Men puff big when Bawitčhuwa is near. I have seen Walks Back Night stretch before Her like a dog wanting scratch, his cockhead blazing. She snaps Her teeth at him and he rolls. If he follows Her, Old Women spit at him.

Bawitčhuwa's Appe promised Her to Rabbit, and when Rabbit died, Her Appe told Her She could choose. All wives hope She chooses not their Husbands.

Men watch Her. Hope for Her. Bring gifts. Fish as long as a short Man's legs. Hunks of Buffalo. Deer hearts. Men lick their lips, say when She has babies, Her milk will drown us all. Her Appe and Bia grow as greasy as fat Bears. Soon they will become as big as Buffalo.

Bawitčhuwa comes to River last. She does what She wants. She perches on juts-over River rock and pulls Her robe off over Her head and stands naked too long forever.

Her skin is River bramble in early Debai-light. Her nest-hair is as sleek and shiny as Beaver.

Old Women splash Water on their ankles and turn to watch young Women and Bawitčhuwa chipping for battle.

Young Women peep Bawitčhuwa, and then turn their backs to Her, hunch their shoulders together, laugh.

Puh, Bia says, Show their want; lose their power.

Women say, Bawitčhuwa's legs are so strong She could squat and grind all day and never tire. Forget good work. Forget children. While She huffs over your Husband, you will work to feed Her. With those big hips, they say, SHE will have so many children we will all starve.

In winter, when food is scarce and the People are hungry I shrink to bones.

Bawitčhuwa never loses fat. Her breasts remain the size of Buffalo balls, firm and high.

Her ass as plump as a Mountain Ram rump.

Puh. She is lazy, my Bia tells me, not the worker you are.

I am dry and hard and skinny. Not like Bawitčhuwa with Her berry-stained fingers, Her plump greasy lips. I have dressed over a hundred animals since we set camp. *Spirit* teeth click in my gut. Crows smack my name in their black leather tongues and call their Brothers to my blood-stiff hair. I wash with River clay and cannot wash stink from my hair.

Look to All, Appe tells me. You are All you see. See All good. Appe opens his arms. See light flitter like Birds on silver leaves. See Beavers, slick as minnows, chew down Trees, and if you are quiet you will see Weta's eyes watching through leafy branches.

Appe places his palm over my eyes. Look inside, he says. See the stories you hold.

I see long back. Night glows brighter than Agai coming up River. Up from Earth, a smell rises from where Pop Pank stands, so sweet, so fullish, blossoms puffing in Budding Season cannot fill my nose. Outside Grass Dance circle, Pop Pank stands so quiet I hear her teeth clicking. I see Men and Women dance for grasses to grow for Deer and Elk, for All animals, for All Fish, for All People. A scent stirs in my marrow. A gut pot boils. A snake hole waggles. The quivering scent of Earth yawns. Grasses writhe up from Pop Pank's River dampness, her red Agai heart. Grasses rise from her small shaking body.

Men fall to their knees, their eyes wurtling round.

Days of *ene'e*

Water is so cold I am breathless. Bia mouths for me to follow and we return to River bank to watch. Bia is trouble-faced. She squints into Water light. She wraps me in my robe and gathers her blanket and together we stand shivering. A deep smell shudders over Waters, sweeps across River in ripples.

I see now what Appe sees. Ogres bob up and then down, Their stony heads sleek and round from Water rub. Women perch on rocks, not rocks, mistaking Ogres for places to rest, not seeing loll of Ogre heads rise between their legs as they lean forward, then back, and kick their feet in Water. Ogres' stony eyes roll as They watch Women bathe, as They wait beneath and beside Water to wed them.

Do you see Them, Bia? All along the Water line?

Bia cups her eyes, and looks. I cannot, she says. Only Earth-close People see Them. The Old and the Young. The Ones given sight.

Mud Squatter plops into the Water and heads to where Water is angry, where giant Ogres cackle at boulders. Water spits white and gurgles round and round Mud Squatter while Women shiver together.

Mud Squatter teases Ogres. I can tell. She smacks her lips at Them and They roll under her waves. Mud Squatter swims where we cannot, where we are afraid, and is happy. She putters and puffs. Her hands paw. Her head bobs in her own splashes.

Debai squints at Mountain edges and we shield our eyes to see Mud Squatter eel across the widest wound of River. She becomes Beaver-sleek past Water so deep, so black, to look there is to become blind.

Far below her, *Spirit* caves chicker with the winking Dead.

When Mud Squatter reaches the far bank, she hefts herself up and rests. She rests for a time too long.

Young Women call to her.

Leave her to herself, my Bia tells them. Can you let old Women rest?

Mud Squatter sits up and pats her face. She cups her hands round her eyes and looks around as if she does not know where she has landed. Far above her, cliffs rise too steep to climb. Mud Squatter s-shakes her naked body and climbs anyway.

Ahhh, my Bia groans.

Mud Squatter taps here and there and slowly makes her way up cliff wall.

Halfway up, Mud Squatter stops to stand where Mountain Goats have stood. Rocks tumble past her, clatter all the way down and splash into River. No one should be where Mud Squatter stands.

Far below her, green Water wriggles, and waits.

Bia fists her mouth. She will fall, my Bia says. That foolish old Woman will fall.

Pop Pank dips beneath River and boils Water with her breathhh.

What is she doing? Bia asks. She should be watching her Gagu, not calling noise to herself. Puh. White Man knew Pop Pank was special but Bia says work is worth.

Mud Squatter grasps at horsetail clumps and climbs higher, higher yet, and comes to top bluff where she hand slaps here there searching for holds.

At last, she fists Bird weed and kicks herself up on the rock shelf and rests.

My Bia taps my arm and points her chin at Bawitčhuwa floating in Water. Bawitčhuwa smiles a River bug smile—knifes her arms and legs—and skims top Water. If Mud Squatter fell, Bawitčhuwa would own the old Woman's Death.

Far above us .. Mud Squatter stands on the edge of the World .. and stretches.

Women back up to the River shallows, their eyes on Mud Squatter, All Women but Bawitčhuwa. Bawitčhuwa stays flow-ting. Smile-ing.

High above us, Mud Squatter's shadow quivers through skinny Trees. When she steps from the shadowy saplings, Debai ticks through tall grasses. Watery blue branches sway as s-s-s-she edges her way out to an overhang thin as a s-snake's tongue.

Women wave their arms. Come back, they shout.

Birds wing beneath the shaley plank Mud Squatter walks upon. Rocks split beneath her feet and plunk|splash to Water. A breeze smokes upward and then dust spittle comes
> down
>> down
>>> and down
>>>> again and
>>>>> scatters over River.

On Earth's crumbly tongue, Mud Squatter stands Weasel-eyed. Woozy. Her breasts wobble as she peaks her hands above her head and smalls herself. She killdeers off the ledge and hits Water like a coup crack, her *Spirit* spraying upward fizzing white. We smell pine-needle hiss of her body before she becomes River.

We wait for her to surface until our dark selves stretch tall. Sky becomes color of clay. Mud Squatter has become only quiet, only sounds of Water lapping and rushing on in ripples.

Ogres wink at us in River light.

Pop Pank smiles and drifts along in swirling Ogre-crackling River bends as if nothing is wrong, as if nothing is wrong at all.

Women slap Water skin and Water rings out. They call her name, her name-no-longer. *Mud Squatter.* Spit sizzles in the pitch of their voices.

Bia holds me as we walk back into Water. We shiver beside one another. We know now. River has taken Mud Squatter.

Bawitčhuwa gathers her robe and leaves as Women begin to wail. But when Men come to River, their eyes wound-dark, Bawitčhuwa waits and watches. Children cry.

Blue Elk runs past all of us. He runs so quickly, leaps from juts-over River rock and spears into River headfirst and I feel the *cedar wind of him passing.*

Appe squats beside River and watches currents looking for any sign of Mud Squatter.

Blue Elk is gone too long and Bawitčhuwa returns to stand on rock Blue Elk leapt from. She disrobes again slowly this time. And as Bawitčhuwa enters Water her breasts float. Her nipples become as large as thimbleberries. Foam gurgles from the mouths of Ogres.

Bia sees *IT* first. Narrow edge of Monster moving through Water, lipping waves. A back hump stirs Women and one after the other Women spin, jump, squeal as Monster threads in and around us.

Bia does not flinch. She grips my hand and makes me stand still beside her.

Blue Elk's breath bubbles to the surface and he emerges like Otter, shakes his head, lifts his hand to other Men before he dips down again into black Water caves.

Look, *look*, Bia says. River dimples with light. S s sw-wirl of swift feet. Beavertail currents. Purled wash of skin. Small bubbles swarm my knees. A large Fish brushes scales against my hand, glints silver past my legs.

Bia cups her hand to my ear—*Mud Squatter*—she whispers. We are not to speak *Mud Squatter's* name, not call her up from River that has claimed her.

Day speak at edges-of-dark

Bia stops working. She sits away from camp, away from firelight and Debai light. I see the old Woman she will become. In the nest-shade of mice and winter Birds, she burrows in dark stickery brush and does not flinch. She behaves like Deer stalked by boys. She will not go to River to bathe.

Women cook for her. Come to stand beside her. I hear Onion Wife's stories riffling beneath wind, striking low rocks, murdling in the tall dry grasses.

Should I beat her from the brush like a sage grouse? I ask Appe.

Do not bother her, Appe says. She seeks herself.

I pound Elk and berries to paste I dry into rounds. I bring Bia seeds and Elk cakes. I wait beside her but she does not eat. She does not talk. Her eyes are unseeing.

Cameahwait brings her steaming liver but she does not sniff.

Stand, I tell her. Walk. If she stays to herself too long, she will be left. They will call her crazy. They will call her Woman Who Sits in Sticker Bush. Debai rises. Nights go. Crows peck her food. Mice rattle beside her. I climb into the bushes and push at her from behind. I grab her hands and pull but she has no grip. Days into days, her face remains as beaten as a fire stick. Pelted. Yelled. She does not move. She is not Bia.

I work for her and for me. I carry her Water. I grind her meal. I scrape her Deer bones. I snare her Rabbits. I carry. I carry her. Many days pass and she grows skinny as Coyote in winter. She is gone.

I go alone now to River. When I step into River hole and splutter and bleat, and go under, light changes and crinkles beneath me. I hear my heart drum .. Far away I hear Bia .. Bia calling .. Bia calling me.

And then Bia is splashing toward me. Bia is moving Water. She is swimming. With one arm stronger than Antelope legs, she pulls me from River dark. She hefts me like a Buffalo leg over her bony shoulder. Everyone turns to look. She falls down and cradles me like Combs Gut cradles Too Ott Lok. Her tears spill over me.

My Baide, Bia cries and cries, My Baide.

I try to stand. I try to push away. I am too old for foolish tears but her grip is fierce.

All night she watches me like a dog eyes a boil pot for drops.

Why does she cry? I ask. I am alive. I am here.

She cries for gone *Mud Squatter*, Appe tells me. Tears are sneaky. They come when we do not want them.

When we go to River Bia watches me. She catches me when I slip on slippery rocks. She follows me tight as blood bugs. When I stretch my arms to yawn, I strike her. Young Bias titter at us while their babies splash in Water.

Pop Pank swims up beside me. I will teach you to swim strong, Pop Pank says. You will not go under.

Pop Pank climbs like squirrel. Spears River waves like Agai. Leaps like Antelope. She is muscly as Agai born of Water. I cannot learn her ways to swim.

Pop Pank slaps my belly, my legs. Make yourself skinny, she says. You will glide like an arrow over waves.

Bia elbows my side. Puh. Do not be stupid and try her tricks. It will get you Dead.

Bia thinks big of me. I would not swim in River shadows. I am afraid of edges-of-dark, afraid of Wood and River Monsters.

Pop Pank lives at the edges, places where we become our most power.

Appe says Pop Pank prepares for the day she will have need to sleep in Water. His eyes become sharp as awls. He knows.

In early light I am. Naked. Chest deep in Water. All Around me reeds are as tall as saplings.

I dig with my toes for bulbs, potatoes, sweet roots. A rush of bubbles floods the surface .. boiling .. boiling .. I stand unmoving .. Let Water clear. Circles lap from Cattails. Calm. Slow. I breathe in and dig again. I have been collecting all day. I have wandered from Bia and removed my robe. Wind carries Bia's voice, her talk, the small sound of her becomes like Birds skimming River hatch. She talks on, not knowing I no longer hear her words.

Between my feet brown stones, clear speckled River rocks. Amber green, the color of Blue Elk's eyes in Sunlight. I look.

A rock looks like a nose? A glint. Fish scale eyes? Light loosens dark reeds. What do I see?

Blood pecks my skin like tiny Birds.

She rises from the silty River bottom where lazy Fish sleep. Her hair snakes the way roots twist in pull-Water.

I drop my basket and run in thick mud, Water gurgle, a bladder push of waves.

I hear laughter.

Come back, Pop Pank says.

When I turn, she is already turning back—turning back—to Water.

I run to camp where nothing has changed. Boys practicing. Men testing.

Women stirring pots. Girls gathering to play.

Walks Back Night runs around and around camp, his Man-push like a knife sticking out below his bloat-gut. All day he runs, runs and runs around camp, jumping over cook fires, bothering Women working. Around again. His Man-push flapping. His humped back shining. How many Rutting Seasons has he plagued us? He is as old as wind and as dry as rocks.

Women watch him with tough eyes and speak behind their hands as he passes.

I have big ears too, he puffs.
Old Women laugh like girls.
I hide in the tall grass where no one can see or hear me.
Pabyhina I whisper there.

Day of everybody laugh good husband

My Appe, Blue Elk, and No Bear Is His Enemy come together. Through the Lodge flap I see them smoking. I see glazed scars, the color of Bawitchuwa's lips, on No Bear Is His Enemy's shoulder.

Bia sits big beside me—snarl-mouthed—as other Women look over from where they work.

Appe, Blue Elk, and No Bear Is His Enemy talk on.

Children shriek and run, stop to stare, then run on.

Soon enough Women leave their work to see what is going on inside our Lodge. Steals Night stands in front of me looking as if I am Water she can see through. She cups her ears. She leans forward.

Go back to your chores, Bia tells Women. There is nothing to see here but my Baide being promised to our greatest Warrior. What do his looks matter to my Baide? What of his power and many honors? Puh. My Baide is strong and can have any Man she wants.

Women gather around me like hair snakes. I feel the nettle of their eyes. The bite sting of their Wombs.

This one, Bia says, bumping my shoulder with hers. Something must be *wrong* with her.

She would rather pound meat or search for mouse beans. She prefers work all day. Puh.

Now see Warrior—great provider Blue Elk—chases *her*.

I lower my head, pull quills through tight teeth. My face prickles. My ear threads

a trace, a blood track of Men and their talk. I hear faint sounds of Water, boiling wind carrying *his* voice. Blue Elk talking to my *father. My Appe.*

I look up and see Pop Pank leap over two small boys.

Men push their heads out of Lodge flaps to see if they should know what.

Pop Pank runs so fast when she stops short River-rain trails her. Run, Pop Pank tells me. Trouble is coming. She speaks in scraps. -ka'ah -kacih -katyn -kepiih.

Pop Pank gets down on all fours and threads through legs of Women.

I warned you, Pop Pank says.

Before Bia has Pop Pank tethered, Bawitčhuwa ruts toward us.

See, Pop Pank says.

Bawitčhuwa snatches up ground at Weta pace. Women gather close as Bawitčhuwa tugs, yank-scalps their hair with fists. Step aside, She cries. *Move.* She spits. She grabs a dead fire stick and waves it at them.

They do not strike back. They know what She has come for. She has come for Blue Elk.

Her greedy-gut blows up air around us like a Water bladder.

I want to run. Bawitčhuwa wants Blue Elk.

Women collected for gossip want blood.

Bawitčhuwa is not interested. We are Birds of no big matter. She yowls for Blue Elk. Her voice claws like dying animals.

Bawitčhuwa turns toward me. Her eyes like Cougar eyes.

Her eyes on me, eyes on me. On me. The vein on Her forehead so big I could pluck it with my thumb and pinch.

Bia wobbles up from ground to stand in front of me. Women titter like seed Birds in Trees. Brings Home Wolf claps her hands. Gut work and sweat glitter like Crow peck spatter on Women's faces.

They circle.

I know to look away. Know not to move.

I stand .. back one .. small step .. from Bawitčhuwa .. as the Lodge flaps opens and Blue Elk steps forward. The bluster sight of him .. stops All .. Everything ..

Everyone ..

Bawitčhuwa pounces Blue Elk and Blue Elk stands as still as sighted Deer. Everyone sees only Bawitčhuwa and Blue Elk now. Those two together. My stomach is Buffalo gut glowing with sour light, scraped out. I am dust that twirls and fades in cross   winds.

Bawitčhuwa's head reaches the curl of his throat. She snatches at him. His skin whitens beneath Her finger grips. Blue Elk does not move. He stands so still I see his skin ripple. Muscle waves twitch over his smooth chest.

No Bear Is His Enemy slips out of our Lodge and leaves like a Fox with Turtle eggs, and when he looks back at his son in the center of Women, he smiles.

Catches Bone steps up beside Bawitčhuwa and pat-pats her back. Come, she says, her voice small.

I think Bawitčhuwa will let go, but She swathes Her arms around Blue Elk's neck so tightly She hangs from him. Her feet. Her body. She has made Herself his Game sack. Hanging. Slack. Spoiled.

Blue Elk has become Deer. His watch on distant sage. Sage powders the air and Blue Elk waits for change. Waits for flinch. For sign. For chance. To leave. To bound   away.

Could it be he cannot see what we all see in Bawitčhuwa? What young Women see?

The gathered Women become stone-faced. Stopped. Stilled.

Blue Elk steps so quickly away Bawitčhuwa clatters to hard ground. A pinch, an awl prick of shame. Only Onion Wife crouches over holding her gut-wheeze of laughter.

Bawitčhuwa made herself ugly with want.

Bia waves her arms to curse Women from Bawitčhuwa. Women laugh .. laugh and
laugh .. and far away They slap each other laughter. *Cackle caw crow.* Their laughter wakes Trees. Hungry *Spirits*.

Bawitčhuwa gathers herself Together. Her blood circling and circling in her veins, in the River of her Life. Her Life bigger than want. She gathers Herself together and becomes all-Women-blood. She becomes a branch struck by Lightning.

She Becomes Here Now Never Gone

She strike me with Her look.

She strike me days worse than Death.

She strike all my children up ahead where I go   away from me.

She strike me gone. Gone to where our People do not go. But even more—

She strike the jittery Stars can never lead me home.

Appe says, Men curse Women with Women.

Men say, Bawitčhuwa is so beautiful we will never know darkness.

Onion Wife says, even in shame Bawitčhuwa shows the power of Women. She says, Men do not know We Women gather ourselves as teepee poles and build new Lodges. We overcome want. What we have is bigger than want. We are the Heart of our People. Jealousy is weak thread that binds nothing.

Bia says, Onion Wife does not know Bawitčhuwa. Puh.

Night morning comes for me

Wake, Appe tells me. Come see.

Appe's face is shadow lit, the face of Rock cliff who has seen many things.

Bia walks beside me, places her fist to her mouth, and we stand. Around us hills rumble and plume. Rising plumes of dust in the Thunder strikes of Horse hooves. I see Bā'bi—my Brother Cameahwait—riding to my Appe, to my Bia, to me. Dust feathers behind Cameahwait, around him   everywhere. Men ride beyond him, toward us. Round and round they come. Down the hill they come. In a wide wide circle they come.

In the kicked dust, I see him—Blue Elk in the middle of their circle—Blue Elk walking to me. On his shoulders he carries Antelope. On his Horse more Antelope. Blue Elk's skin is the color of smoked hide, smooth as River wash. Shining. His hair is long and so black each strand echoes blue, liver blood. He comes toward me, cool of River Canyons, night red fires, wind of Trees, dust smoke.

He comes toward me in the center of day-ever-same.

In the rise-dust, People gather. In the Horse circle, Men yip. Women trill.

Blue Elk places Antelope before Appe. Blue Elk gathers his Horses and ties them
beside our Lodge.

No one speaks.

My Bia sets her chin to chest and gulps air.

My Appe lifts my hand palm up and Blue Elk places his hand over mine. He is tall over me, tall as Tree shadow.

Moon rises over Trees .. River Ogres gurgle. Women mouth my name. How can this be?

Bawitčhuwa cursed me to : : second ugly wife, cursed me to lost children : to an old Husband who squats behind me.

Now Blue Elk plucks me. I am a ripe summer Prairie. I am the berries of distant Mountains only *Sacred Weta* eats. Blue Elk is my age and then half my age again. He is a young Man, a Warrior, with long days ahead.

I am a mouse shaking in the tatter leaves.

Night of too soon dark

Tonight my People dance and the dance goes on. Trough fires burn into star smoke night.

I squat in bushes to piss and hear grunting Man. Patter of his piss on leaves. A yellow creek runs toward me. I make no sound. I find wet grass .. soft leaves .. Weta quiet .. Deer and Elk and Moose quiet.

On distant bluffs surrounding camp, shadows of Men crouch in grass. They are not Walk-Around-Watchers. While we danced, Enemy gathered around us. While we celebrated, Enemy waited in darkness. I hold my breath and run to Appe.

Appe whistles smoke through his teeth, screech-hoot, gathers his arrows, and heads to where I hid from Man. From Enemy.

If we must leave, Bia says to my Brother Cameahwait, Come back here. Take your Sister down to River where Sweetgrass grows. Hide and we will find you.

Bia takes my hand. Cameahwait follows Appe.

We won't stay inside Lodge, Bia says. She sits on her haunches and pulls me down beside her.

When Bia was young, her Lodge was knifed open while she slept. Her Sister was wounded. Her Bia too. Now she no longer waits in Lodges at threat of Enemies. She has told other Women her fear has made her strong.

Women crouch in bushes with children. Always Alone holds her hand over baby's mouth.

We wait in darkness together, apart.

When Moon s-laughter-s clouds, Bia throws a robe over my head. I peer through a small opening when I hear hollow thunks of arrows hitting trees. One flaming arrow charges Sky. I listen to rounds of arrows released. In the place where I squatted arrows rain down. At far edge of camp, one arrow sizzles in grass and catches fire.

Bia holds me close. We hear a hundred bait teeth snaps. Branches crack. Voices rumble.

Men whoop laugh. Men shadows rise tall in the wake of small fire.

They found Dodges Woman walking the rim of camp. A watcher. A protector.

It was nothing, the Warriors say. Only fear-chatter of young Woman afraid of the dark.

Only me.

Women gather green robes to snuff out flames. Bia stands tall and wraps her robe around my shoulders. She hisses at me behind tight teeth.

See the trouble you caused, Baide? On a good night with good All Around you. On the night you are claimed by our great Warrior, you cause trouble.

Look, Bia says, Blue Elk walks toward us. See. I told you. No one wants a trouble girl. But a great Warrior? Puh. Dishonor scours his face.

Blue Elk threads through quivering grass. Warrior quiet. Weta quiet. Starlight tips Mountains blue and All become one. River fields and Stream shine and Animal shiver and his black hair, All blue. I see his breath smoke like the thinnest strands of silver gut. He stops before me and lifts his torch above my head. I am the Fish he catches now. I tatter in light that spills from his neck bone to his ankles. Torch light. Blue Elk light. The light of Warriors. His body is an arrow, his Man-push hard against his breechclout.

Appe—drunk with War fires—grabs my shoulders. My Baide is dreaming of Men pissing in bushes, he says. She is almost ready for you, Blue Elk.

Bawitčhuwa stands at edges-of-dark. Her rancid eyes glower at me. She punches me with her eyes. She belches Skunk Death and Bird claw. She counts coup with her coup stick of bone.

Puh. She is less than mice chew, Bia tells me.

Bia does not know All fear. She does not know Women whispered behind their hands and called her crazy when she slept in bushes. She forgets that once our Women clobbered Enemy Women, and scalped them alive. If Bawitčhuwa is less than mice chew, she is the Vole that climbs up Enemy ass. She is the Sick at the edges-of-dark.

Men search fields and find no Enemy in grasses. No Enemy Horses. No Enemy Horse plop. No One. They find only Owl-scared Rabbits, scudder of Voles, and Dodges Woman, who stands guard all night and walks the rim of camp to watch. Dodges Woman is a new Night Watcher. He is young and wants to be a great Warrior. I fear I have shamed Dodges Woman.

You will bring him your best basket filled with berry-pounded meat, Bia tells me. You will cook for him at Debai wake.

Deep in my body a baby Bird sleeps. She flitters up and away from my trouble. Away from Womb ache, and rage. My bones are light as Muskrat bones. My teeth are small as Rabbit teeth. I quake under Buffalo robes so heavy my ribs bow. Beneath the Womb-glow Moon, Enemy Warriors swim downstream and wait for us, their breath wheezing through reed holes.

Day of not-spoken

The story is ugly, Bia tells me, when we are alone in the Womb-dark haze of Mother talk. We stand beside fire's roar, snap of wood, whoop of smoke, where even Weta sharp ears cannot hear. Here, Bia protects me from Bawitčhuwa spatter.

You are old enough to know Onion Wife lost her Baide to three Men who once were good.

Bia crouches, tugs me to Earth, where dust powders our hands. Bia shakes grass around us, lights sage, and Smudges me.

One day you will hear the story from Onion Wife herself but I tell you now so her words cannot harm you. What I tell you will wake you to All Around .. ..

To wake to All Around means my story will change you from now into on. You have been all along dreaming. What you know to be Beautiful is Ugly. You will see blood traces of the Dead on rose thorns where you gather food. You will know what you have not been told. You will see liars and thieves you once thought were good.

Bia covers my shoulders in grass .. I hear her heart drum ..

River voice settles. Bia's voice falls to dust and smaller sounds rise. Mint whispers beneath dry brush. Moon clouds powder Sky. Mice rustle so close Milk pods jickle .. jickle jickle jickle. Muskrat scritters in marshy Water gnawing splinter caps.

When Bia speaks again her words wobble on rain-beaten rocks. She calls upon the power of her tongue. Bia becomes long-ago Song, bigger, wider, All Around. She chants in the ways of Women to keep Men away.

Three Men brought back a wasteful devouring *Spirit*. Bia spits. They brought bad dreams of what is yet to come from far-up River. Because we are Agai People, Bia says, bending low, we feel change along Water lines. Bia flaps her arms like she is Crow flying over Water.

I feel transformation. In the deep coiled grasses and in the places we sniff, but do not enter, Debai trickles downward, and the smell of what has been, and what will come, turns poison.

Three Men, who became not-our-own, carried tatters back to us—scalp-flesh torn from young Women, *Spirit* meat hiss, their cock-stink abomination. They were not War party, not Hunt party, not scouts. They brought back nothing, not even themselves.

Bia's story is sticky in the telling. Each word latches her tongue. Her story has become a difficult journey.

They attacked White Crow as if she were Enemy. They broke her wide open, tore her Womb. Puh, she says, White Crow became less than Marten tongue, less than unlicked bone.

Bia fastens her eyes on the grind-stone Moon. River flushes the watery color of rinsed blood.

Listen, my Baide, even stones hear what I am saying. What happened to White Crow has given ugly ways a path to all Women. Now *men* with War eyes—with pouches of broken teeth and scalp-ripped flesh at their hips, with fingernail-Moon-gouged arms, and no-good stink of Women used .. *men* with nothing to pour their seething into, but Women, see Women .. as less than, and return to us hate. Hate, an infection, never before and unforeseen, and now All Around and coming. More and more hate come. Like craziness, hate come. Like Badger foaming mouth, hate come. Like *men* at War with nothing, hate come .. Like Flatbird's vision of White Men swarming Rivers, hate come.

Like stingers in the ribs of dead Buffalo who no longer recognize Death, *men* come.

Bia's words are stick pokes, must-listen words, gut speak of Women to heal, to call back,
to make right what has been wronged.

Used to be Water Babies were our only Monsters. Water Babies who called Women to their Deaths. Now *War* men are our Monsters. *War-men*-want glistens on Women like pinecone sap at Debai rise. Crazy-want walks up River, up from the maggot hearts of *men* who have become what they should not become. *men* who let their War stink invade our Sacred Lodges, our Sacred openings.

Women must find the path for our People to go on.

Remember what I am telling you, my Baide. We Women can shatter rocks with our anger. We can pound Earth and call up broken Womb-heart of Women or we can call *must-not-be-named*.

Onion Wife called *must-not-be-named*. Not our Women-blood. Not our gut power. Onion Wife hurled *must-not-be-named* upon the sons of the men who gouged White Crow, who split her and beat her, and broke her, and left her Dead.

must-not-be-named, Bia whispers, is a *Spirit* of this Earth that even *Wolf* cannot name, a *Spirit* we cannot leash or tend.

These men brought great and terrible to us.

Onion Wife brought rage that trembles around us like wounded Enemy.

Bia places her hand beneath my chin. Bawitčhuwa eyes you like Wolf eyes Hunter with fresh meat. I see her. Waiting. Wanting.

must-not-be-named rattles along Rivers beside her want.

Wind snips and flaps our robes. I tell you this, my Baide, to prepare you. You must watch for Tricksters of all kinds, my Baide. Do not trust easy ways. *must-not-be-named* dangles before us like good. Like easy. Like always Trickster. We are small beside Earth stories.

Spiders spin sticky twine beside me, their silver thread catches light. Bia swipes my hair.

Sleep is a Badger snuffling outside the skin of our Lodge. The Horses Blue Elk gave paw the ground close to my head .. Shudder .. Flinch .. Flap their tails. I smell blood bladders, roil of Horse piss.

I see shadows of Women .. shadows of *bowel-Spirit Women.*
Shadows of Enemy Women.

Hot shiver-snorts of Horses come at me like War Men. Horses paw, their stone-sharpened hooves too close to my skull.

I am both awake and asleep. Moon spears through tule mats to find my feet Rabbit-twitching, my breath clibbing like a small Bird's heart clibs in my hand before Death. I hear sounds *Walking Trees* make as They move through Moon skin nights. When *Walking Trees* uproot and walk, They sing in the shadowy forests, and we hear Birds.

Do all things lie?

ka-*wit* ka- *wit*

ka-*wit* ka- *wit*

Horse piss yellow as Moon light leaks beneath my Buffalo robe, and wets me.

I clean myself outside, alone, in the hour of whimpering Horses, in night-of-always-now, in the needle-sharp score of needle Trees walking.

I listen. All night Bia's words are hot as cooking rocks.

I sleep the sleep of stones. Deep. Dreaming. In night's dark rattly breath, animals scritter around me. Monsters and Men who become Monsters. Stone Ogres coming out of Their stone caves to watch Women. Ogres who want only to save us.

I wake to bundles tied on the shorn manes of Blue Elk's gifts. One Horse blinded. His tail stripped to bone, mane cut to blood. Someone wants Blue Elk cut from me.

I know what I am.

I am the one Bawitčhuwa sends *bad Spirits, the Devil, must-not-be-named.* Small snorts from her wound-Womb. All Around me.

Day of ~~clean~~ sing

Atawatchi puffs smoke from his lungs, a Stream so thin it whistles the low whistle of snakes before striking. His smoke s-s-lips sl-its bush and shadow grasses-s. Bawitčhuwa's smile drifts away.

Smoke rises from camp—blue claws of smoke rise to—call *White Weta*.

Smoke Smudge centers me. Becomes the center of me.

In blue smoke I am lit.

In blue smoke I am lit.

In bark smoke of Atawatchi's prayers. I see Agai River gleam.

Appe pulls me to edge of Atawatchi's circle. There, he says. Can you see them, my Baide? Enemy all around?

I see dense trunks of Trees close to Water.

Yes, he tells me. Look there. Closer.

Little by little Enemy moves toward us, he says.

I look where Appe points and scat-scattered darkness becomes Men crouched in fields, in grassy Deer beds, in hill cracks.

When I look again I see nothing.

Atawatchi shakes his head. It is beyond, far beyond us, he tells Appe. We cannot chase what-will-be.

A *bad Spirit* comes:

Appe will not go with other men to hunt. All day he haunts fields and tall grasses. Early day, he digs a hole for himself at camp edge. Early night, he rubs his skin with dirt. Appe's eyes are crazy, moving the way Antelope hops, jumpy at noises no one hears. He knows what I fear. I fear change coming.

All day, all night Appe watches nothing at all.

Atawatchi prays for him now for he sees what we do not.

Atawatchi says we need a Ceremony for all the People.

Flatbird listens.

I wait ..

Day will come, Appe tells me, when you will see differently. Days will no longer be alive to you. You will olden, my Baide. What remains is what you have learned, what you take with you from Here.

Keep Here. Be Here. He knocks on my chest with his knuckles and my heart quickens.

Know bad day will come, he said. Prepare.

Day of many days of want

Blue Elk left as Sun dulled Sky—*Spirit Sky*—in the hour of
first feeding. Animals turn colors of dust. I am as colorless as Turtle
shell, gristle, pocked bone, butchered mouths. I rise and collect myself the way tree seeds collect. I look toward Budding Season when
seeds become the breath of Trees after winter.

Appe says, We know the length of our days before each day
comes. In the waking hour
we are fizzing breath, edge of animal sleep, and if we stay still we
will hear ourselves return to our skins.

Animals shiver in shiver grass of Blue Elk's leaving. He has
gone to scout for Enemy. He has gone to honor me. Blue Elk's
Horse knows ways of Mountain Goats and steps so no Enemies
can hear.

While other Hunters sleep, Blue Elk reaches the cool dark of
high rock overhangs. His Horse sidesteps the slittering snores of
quiet snakes. His shoulders wrapped in Weasel skins, his waist bare
and sleek. His skin is the color of red stones. His nose is fine-boned
as Deer Woman. He keeps his face close to Horse's head as he rides
toward coming winter quiet as blue snake.

Blue Elk, his wood-dark eyes, his guarding lashes, will have
many wives. I will be first.

This I know. No one holds another.

He sees Deer herd asleep in frost grass and hunts Men he cannot see. He cannot see the me I become. A soon-wife with many
responsibilities.

Bia says my eyes wander too much. She says she can see my want
for travel, to be as far away as Warriors who hunt Men. She is not
wrong. I want to travel like Agai back to my birthplace.

Wind rushes down Mountains and blows our scent to animals.
Deer, Antelope hide from us now. We have stayed so long we have

lost the ability to smell our own kill smell. Black flapping Birds
carry our names to their Brothers.
Our time of gathering *here* is over.
Our time of dancing *here* is over.
It is the Season to pack, to carry, to take away.
Now is the end of Gathering .. We have done what
must be done.

First day of many bad days

The last time I saw Appe alive, he was crouched near first fork of River. His eyes wild looking here, looking there, toward hills, toward River bank that flanked us. Appe startled again and again. He became Deer with kill hooves skittering for Life; he shoved me to hard ground. My legs burned in the crush of sting weed. A *bad Spirit* had found us.

I became the Fish that tricks other Fish, stunned and flapping on the ground, calling out to River. I heard sounds of a thousand bees grinding the still air above me.

Bad day had come.

Far down Valleys white moths quivered above fields. I looked toward camp. Bia unmoving. Women and old Men stopped work to listen.

Earth rumbled. My legs began to tremble, then shake. Buffalo .. Not Buffalo .. Enemy.

Men rode toward us from all sides.

Old Women shrieked. Children cried. Dust plumed down Mountains scattering dirt clods. A Man I did not know pitched forward over the head of his Horse and his black mouth opened to dirt as red Horse clattered over him.

And then I was running. Black-tailed Deer quivered beside me bounding toward River. I ran beside Deer before Deer cut to hills. The lungs of a great animal gathered wind behind me. Hooves hacked Earth.

I threw my hands up in gusts of Horse's pass. My scalp hissed. Slick-face Enemy halted Enemy Horse. His sweat stench circled me. He laughed and fisted a thin tail of my hair over his head.

I scrambled up River cliffs where dirt gave way to roiling sand and fell into galloping Water. River churned bubbles as if a thousand silver Birds were flapping at my head, twirling me end over end over end. Far below, giant rocks as greasy as Bear bones pulled River down to green, then black, and I was sinking sucked beneath dark bellies of boulders so huge families of *Spirits* gathered beneath them. Ogres chuzzled my sinking body. Nickering.

Horse swam far above me, yellow Water foaming in the churn of His legs.

. I was free.

Powder Moon drifts in Sky. My Bia's huckleberry-stained hands comb my hair. For a Lightning strike I am among my People. Breath-less. And then I am leaving. My *Spirit* whiffling. Tamarack smoke lifts me. Dark *Wolf* stands on the hill, ready to call me away. Elders say, Death is *to be taken* from the place that homes us, and released into Stars.

Currents rushed me to low ground. Horse rattled wetness from its bones and in the Water sting of Horse's shaking, in the slap-swish of Horse's tail, I was alive. As Enemy reclaimed his Horse, he lost his breechclout. His buttocks clenched Horse's sleek belly and Horse turned wild, spinning and bucking in shallow Water, hooves spitting rocks.

Earth slowed as Enemy leapt toward me, Enemy's cock a raised fist. He grabbed me with might force. My head cracked his chest again, again, again, my bones a raid of lights as he thumped thumped against me. I bled a Woman bowl of ache. I called out to Blue Elk. But Blue Elk did not answer my call.

When Enemy finished, he threw me sideways on his Horse and then we were running. Ground swayed beneath us—up and then down. My stomach spilled; ground heaved. We stopped at the End of the World.

Strange Enemy Men gathered beside us. My blood calling them. My wound a gash.

Otter Woman was tied to the back of another Enemy Horse, her body limp, still as Deer meat. Her head bled a River down Horse's side. I heard others crying. I tried to kick off Horse but was bound by Enemy fists. Enemy Rider slapped my buttocks. And all Enemy laughed.

I smelled Death. Last shudder of liver and teeth, bone stink of scalps. I named our Dead: Stands Down Thunder .. Stony Dog's Hair .. Water Comes to Blood .. Flights Flint .. Smoked Lodge .. Smoked Lodge .. my Appe. I saw the long black whip of Smoked Lodge's hair. I would have reached to touch my Appe, claim his scalp if I could. I snapped at Smoked Lodge with my teeth to catch one strand of Appe's hair so he would travel with me.

What was it I saw then? Sky stuttering with light? Trees overhead bending toward me?

No. What I knew to be beautiful was ugly.

My line of sight was Men.

Enemy Men.

Men above and around me. Touching me. Clapping me.

Enemy Horse charged forward.

Lumpy hills throbbed in my heart as Enemy hand covered my face.

STOLEN
THREE FORKS TO MANDAN

Days of Enemy ache

When Sun splits through Trees, I search for wedge rock, whip branch, sting grass, skull weed, Rattler nest, poison stem, shitting grass. I search for Land dips, crumble rocks, Rabbit holes hidden by grass swirls, all places hooves stumble—all things I can use.

Tree lines thicken, then thin.

I scout for open Land, for bothersome Birds that trouble Buffalo, circles of Birds circling Death. Anything that tells me where we are going and how far I am from Blue Elk.

I listen to Wind, if He growls or whistles, if Earth bows to soft bluffs or strikes rocky cliffs, if Wind trammels high branches, or curdles, slows, or quickens. Sound maps the Land.

Drum of hooves clatter on Earth. I mark how far, how close we are to Water. Wind dips and rises like Antelope. I listen the way Appe taught me to listen.

We travel through woods that have not seen fire. Scent of mint needles through Trees. I smell dried wild roses, huckleberry-choke-cherry plop. Elk horn rubs. Animal blood.

I watch .. I wait .. I listen

I see *Weta. Weta running behind. Weta following.*

We travel Elk trails lit in Moon light before Enemy moves back into black stumbling. Trees and thatch hide us. Enemy hides from Blue Elk and Cameahwait, from our many Warriors who will come for us and beat Enemy down like field Birds.

They have tied me to a Tree. Bark chews my back.

Every night Enemy removes a *Spirit Bundle* cinched in Moose skin.

It takes three Enemy to wrestle and retie *It*. At night *It* makes sounds. Sometimes *It* screams. Is this their Ogre *Medicine*? What *It* is moves in darkness, thumps against *It*s leather cage.

How can we beat Enemy with a *Spirit Bundle* as big as a Man's torso?

In smoky light, I see the Taken—my Relations—my People slumped beside Trees. Toyapi, Keeps Lost Horse, Knife Grass, Gwaču, Traders Daughter. Otter Woman lies still beside small campfire. Her face glows with her own heat shine. She is alive or they would have left her, and yet, she is stone. Un-woken.

I watch and wait. All Around they gather sticks and brush and soon all Enemy gathers beside a Monster fire. Flames lick Skyward like dancers. I feel the scorch. If they are not careful, they will light the woods on fire. Enemy is not afraid. They laugh. Tell big stories. Red coals their backs, shadows their bodies. Firelight pitters their faces so they become not themselves. They become the black hearts of War Men. Fire glares on their legs and shines through their big grinning teeth.

I do not understand their words. I understand the language of Big Talk. I understand Thunder of War Men thumping their chests. Mean laughter.

Moon shudders tall grasses. *Spirits* chitter. Badger waddles. Night Birds swoop down, up.

I hear the snarling lick of *Weta*.

Enemy Rider weaves through grasses. In the blind night far from fire. Far from help. My body is a bone sack. Enemy Rider covers my mouth and rides me like his Horse, like Enemy Woman, not a girl who has not bled. My blood shouts. I bleed not Womb blood but captive blood.

Night too soon gone

Before Sun light, I am lifted back on Enemy Horse. They ride quickly now. I do not fall asleep but dreams scatter my thump-thick head.

When I feel heat on the backs of my legs I know we have ridden into day. They have captured Too Ott Lok. He is cry-cr-cry-ing. His crying shimmers the way eyes shimmer before Death.

Combs Gut would not have let go of Too Ott Lok. I am only dreaming.

I open my eyes. With Debai so bright light rings. I keep my head up like a snake and sniff plum and bull berries, the oily scent of Badger. I hold my head up until my sight no longer thumps. I hear Too Ott Lok. No one cries like Too Ott Lok. I wiggle to loosen the ties on my hand. If I push forward I can see .. his neck the color of plums .. his face the color of Water plump potatoes.

Too Ott Lok? Enemy grabbed Too Ott Lok?

It would be a thing to laugh if I did not know Enemy will tire of Too Ott Lok. *We* tired of Too Ott Lok.

Too Ott Lok moans.

When Moppo follow with their stinging winds, blood fat with Enemy blood, Enemy will cut Too Ott Lok like a lump of cattered meat, cut him like curl-gray nests filled with mean stingers. Enemy will cut him from us.

No one shields Too Ott Lok as Horses plunge through brush, swat Trees, poke sticks. Green-thorn branches fling, swat back into Too Lok. Too Ott Lok's face is an awl-punctured hide. He is jabbed so deep he does not bleed. I have seen white bloat fever. His spittle threads silver and shining like spider web.

We travel through moss-grass, mud Waters left from rain. We travel where blood-stingers feed and bloom. Soon all stingers will be gone. Now they are in their last Season feed. I call out. Moppo rise to save us. Come up from Watery places, up from marsh tubers, up from rocks who bowl fists of rain, up from mint grasses.

I call to you. Moppo! Come!

Blood-stingers flicker. Moppo. Moppo. A shiver beast. A growl hum. Black nest. Come. Come. Come. Come. Cluster Too Ott Lok. Cloud him. Turn him gray with your storm. Cover sweat-ripe Enemy Rider. Flame HIM with your stingers.

Enemy has not known trouble like Too Ott Lok. His Bia's milk-blood thrums to all tiny creatures who nest in stink Water, Tree rot, all buzzers in ribs of No-longer-living. A raid. A thousand glitter enemies in the mouths of our Dead. *Our Dead*. Rise to help us. River Tree fluff, Milkweed down, Cattail gloss. I hear your Song, Moppo.

Enemy Horse flinches and quails and then skitters sideways. Flies and blood-stingers and black-yellow stingers swirl Enemy's head. Enemy slaps his face and claps his legs to Horse but Horse only turns and turns to nip at swirls of bugs.

Enemy sees Too Ott Lok is his plague, and shoves him, as Enemy Horse lurches and haunches. Too Ott Lok is caught in the fall, in the tangle of buckskin ties, in the wild whipping reins of Enemy. Enemy Horse is galloping now with Enemy and Too Ott Lok. I arch, lift myself as far as I can, and see Too Ott Lok's head bumping Earth. Dust plumes.

Too Ott Lok needs our help. Too Ott Lok, I yell. I battle. I strike Enemy Rider.

Too Ott Lok Too Ott Lok, Others call, my Battle Companions, my Taken, my Own. *Too Ott Lok*, we yell. We scream.

I hear struggle. I hear the battle cry of those too young to wed, too young to name, crying to their Bias, crying to Too Ott Lok. *Too Ott Lok*. Unmoving. Plop sack. Only quiet.

Horse flies scratch our sweat. No cry will wake Too Ott Lok but my chest heaves when I hear the cry of Others.

Out of day's dark, I hear clip, clip, clip of fast Horse. Not-seen-before-Enemy leads a riderless Horse. He is as beautiful as Bawitchwa. He is Beautiful Enemy, taller than other War Men. This Enemy Warrior is muscly as an Elk and moves like Mountain Cat, quietly, stalking. He lifts saggy Too Ott Lok as if Too Ott Lok is as light as an empty root sack. Enemy surrounding us bow to Beautiful Enemy as He cross-ties Too Ott Lok to the riderless Horse. Horse dances sideways, backwards, and Too Ott Lok's arms flop. Flies rise up, light on his swollen face, his gone-eyes.

Enemy Rider reties my hands. Blood beats in my fingers like a drum. I cannot bear Enemy Rider's breath steam as he leans down and nips my ear with his broken teeth. Enemy breath over me, around me, as he pushes me close to Enemy Horse's neck. My body rocks and he slaps his hand to my back and blood lurches in me.
We They move on. Too Ott Lok's body drums, drums Enemy's riderless Horse. I cry for my old meanness to Too Ott Lok that I cannot cut.

Too Ott Lok traveled with Women far into Mountains where huckleberries grow so thick, *Weta* did not bother us.
Too Ott Lok ate so many berries, he shat his self. Combs Gut splashed his butt with drink Water.
Poor Too Ott Lok, Combs Gut said, he is too sick to walk back to camp. You take him back, Combs Gut told us, her crooked mouth pointed at me and Otter Woman.
Bia could not help me. We will get no work done here with him, she told me. Take him back to camp.
Otter Woman clicked her tongue against her teeth and emptied her basket into Bia's. She stepped beside me and we laced our fingers together and Too Ott Lok sagged into our dog-sled arms. We carried him step by step down steep Mountain side, over cold

creek Waters, up and over Tree-falls. Lazy Thing did not make one move to stand. Stink-heavy Too Ott Lok. We lugged him like pull dogs until we were far from Comb Gut ears. And dropped him.

We shredded grass between our teeth as we waited for him to move. We plastered his blister thighs with Bear grease mashed with arrowroot and Heavy Thing sat.

Otter Woman and I began to walk.

Too Ott Lok ordered us like Chief to pick him up.

For a long way down Mountain, we heard his cries.

Carry me, he shouted.

Walk yourself, Otter Woman shouted back.

We stopped. Listened. We heard sluffing footsteps, groans, and here come Too Ott Lok, his fire-stick thighs rubbing together blister-blue as the underside of a dog tongue.

We switched his legs with stinging branches, laughed until he cried loud and louder.

We promised to leave him far behind. One day.

Be careful, my Appe told me, when he heard I switched Too Ott Lok. You must dig out meanness, my Baide, before it comes back round, and stays.

Debai gashes branches of Trees, splits roots of grass. My eyes are as swollen as a Woman-slit before birth.

Night comes to Woods we travel through. I hear sounds of Water and am pulled from Enemy Horse and dropped. To Earth. Dropped to black night.

I listen for my stolen Brothers and Sisters.

Wood Spirits gather here. Trees reach toward each other. In the bristle-smolder of nümü pahamittsi, the *Spirit of Woods*, darkness widens.

In dark night of Enemy sleep

Appe taught me about Weta, about their abilities, their ways.

Antelope and Deer move without sound and fade to yellow in summer grass. Winter Antelope become raw Earth, nothing but Smudge-stain on snow-burrowed hills. They are smart but Weta is wise, Appe told me. Weta protect their young by rustling in brush. They pound the ground with their paws or move without noise.

When Weta leaves, you will know if they want you to know. Earth shakes when Weta runs. When Weta's footsteps Thunder toward you, pray. Weta can slink away smaller than dust-rise. When Weta make themselves known to you, they want you to know.

We are pitiful pickers. When our fingers grope only berry stain, Weta roars up to laugh at us.
Know, Baide, Weta is always laughing at our pitiful ways. Weta knows us well.

I feel the drum of Enemy Horse beneath my beaten ribs. My People's ripe old knowing rides beside me as Enemy Horse moves on and on farther from my People.

Appe led me into shelter Woods care-fully, sl-o-w-ly, as Debai shifted with our steps, Tree by Tree   Branch by Branch   Twig by Twig   Leaf by Leaf.
Freckles of Sun spattered here   there.

When the black Trees held only slivers of light, when Debai stood still above us, Appe—as quiet as an ancient Tree—reached for my hand.

At first We Stood. Stopped.

Appe pressed my hand to his chest. His heart thump slowed. Appe moved with Earth, with Trees. Appe moved without moving, and when he tipped his head toward me I knew stillness, just before, just after each heart .. beat .. Appe's eyes looked but only to shift more light toward me, a gather of Mountain light, seed light. He was looking and not looking at me.

In stillness before and after .. each .. heart drum .. hazy light nested above us in mossy high branches. A deep smell was rising up up up. Breath of Trees and Animals. Walled scent of blue Rivers, biting whiff of onions and rattle bush.

I smelled the silver-lichen Moon.

Appe capped my head with his hand and pointed my sight toward stillness. Late day squinted through Trees. I felt drum .. damp Earth .. spongy twigs roll to dirt beneath our feet. The smallest sounds. The smallest movements in pipsissewa and Rabbit bush. Leaves trembled in air float-ing Water .. No branches held them. Pinecones hung from nothing   as *Spirit* lifted them.

Trees breathed in .. and puffed out .. yellow wind. Great clouds of yellow dust pulsed upward and splintered Sky. Yellow wheeshed the Birds. Appe's face creased with pollen. My braids turned to tallow and Appe became old before my eyes.

Wind creaked through Trees and light throbbed. Debai passed us, shifted shades of Trees and Trees groaned. But it was not Wind through Trees. The Trees themselves were moving. Pine needles bowed, then dropped in sleep. Trees swelled and grew fat with the dusky-sour scent of *Weta*. Chokecherry eyes moved .. glinted. I saw then what Appe wanted me to see.

Weta surrounded us. Weta in low brush. Weta peeked between leaves. A small Weta pawed my feet. A dusty bia Weta stood and sniffed.

Appe pulled my arm. We stepped back, not lifting our feet, stepping back at a Stinkbug's pace and Weta became less and less with little distance from them. Only our looking had changed. Saplings shifted. Colors moved. Weta disappeared.

They always see us, my Appe said. We only see them when they want us to see them. We are like Weta. We hold the gifts of Earth because we are Earth and Water.

We are Agai People. We are Agai Eaters. Weta follows us.

In the dark, Too Ott Lok snorts, his head battered into wounded sleep, sleep without dreams, without voices. I dream the dream of old days. I have left Too Ott Lok behind.

Weta has disappeared.

Days of our Enemies

How many days have passed since capture?

Weta crackles through bristle grass. Peeps at us when Enemy stops for Water. Bounds beside us far enough away Enemy does not see. The farther we get from our camp, Enemy slacks. They are safe to build bigger and bigger fires. Safe enough from Blue Elk and Cameahwait. They do not know *Weta* has come.

Enemy, dizzy with stolen children, drunk with rape, sweat like Women when they scrape-work Buffalo hides. Enemy War-stink titters around us. I cannot look at them when they stare at me. Their eyes glitter dangerous as blind Water.

In their drip sweat, in their boast night, they do not see *Weta*. *Weta* squats in low nest brush as they settle to night.

I see side-glint footsteps. Someone shines in darkness. Not-seen-before Beautiful Enemy—weaves through hip-stiff grasses toward me .. mes-mer-izing snake .. ready to curl, to strike. I prepare myself this time. I call to Bia. I call to Appe.

I remember arrow-hearted cries of Warrior brokenness. Men come back to us changed like They are Trees charred by Lightning and standing without Life.

I have not seen this change before, Bia and Appe said. Warriors no longer our own. Our prayers do not work for them. Child's laughter does not heal them.

I remember Onion Wife's stories of War Men—not Warriors—return after battles. War Men seething. Scorched, she said. Their bodies crooked by stabs, gouged by knife wounds, bulged by liver Death. War Men blind to Women and Children. War Men who only love the stink of each other's asses.

Onion Wife taught Women to fear them.

You should know, Onion Wife said, War Men return like Rams for Women to splay us open. To split our Wombs. To them we are Woman hole, Womb-en, Fish mouth to be bloodied by Enemy fingers. They wish our Life bladder to be gutted, Dead.

Women can be Enemy in their own camps, Onion Wife warned. All Women can be taken like White Crow.

Men who are at-the-edges—Men who are always at War and near Death—seek Life. Our Life. They seek our Womb. Listen to what I tell you. When captured Women hear War Men's head-to-head bone clunk, they know to run, to hide.

I cannot hide. My eyes steam like Rivers after rain.

Is it Beautiful Enemy who squats beside me and pats my hands?

I look into edges-of-dark, into blue dusk, and remember White Man.

Transformations happen at dusk, He said. Along the dusty goat trails leading over cliff edges, in the darkened woods and wide-open Prairies where cloven hooves trod paths, and just beneath water where the river swirls and eddies to collect dead things, look for the things that transform. Somethings transform to holiness; somethings transform into evil.

Beautiful Enemy who was Enemy Warrior, who was wide-shouldered as a Bull Elk, who was taller than all Enemy Warriors is now *Woman*, small as peck seed. Nothing is left of Beautiful Enemy. *She* has eaten *Him*.

|He is woman| pulls my robe up slowly, carefully, in the way Bia lifted the Lodge flap for a sleeping little one.

She gasps at what *She* sees.

|He is woman| runs Bawitčhuwa-like back to *Her* Horse and pulls a bolt of white from *Her* parfleche. White buckskin flags behind *Her* and lights the dark woods.

She returns puffing.

She cuffs *Her* hand to *Her* chest when *She* squats and as |He is woman| lifts my robe I squeeze my eyes shut. I will not let this story in. This is the story I push away. At night Enemy Rider grinds-scrapes-pummels me. I boulder my legs and feel the tear of me, smell the blood wet of me, the White Crow of me between my legs. Between my legs, I have been murdered there.

No more no more no more no more no more no more, I say.

Little one, |He is woman| says. I listen then. Did *She* speak White Man's language?

|He is woman| gazes at me and lifts my robe, again. Higher.

I cannot take another Bull mount. I am cracked open. I knee. I kick.

Weta .. *lifts her head from tall grass* .. *and sniffs.*

I am met with only Milkweed down, a softness like Water silt.

|He is woman| squeals when *She* sees the blood-nest of my crotch. *She* closes my legs and lowers my robe back down. *She* places *Her* hand to *Her* chest and digs in *Her* belt pouch. I feel a tiny drop of Water on my leg.

When |He is woman| cuts me from Tree, *She* moves quickly. I hear *Her* breath ..

breath .. breath .. I feel cool mint leaves and try to lift myself, but cannot.

|He is woman| holds me to *Her* shoulder and wraps buckskin round my ribs and up between my legs. I hear *Her* tongue seethe against *Her* teeth. Seeeetheeeth like a Woman at the pitch of Birth.

Oh, you poor poor little one, *She* says. I hear the sound of White Man words come back in *Her* mouth.

Who is this Enemy? I look. Up close. I look.

|He is woman| painted not for War, but pretty for show, pretty for prance. *Her* cheeks are flush with berry juice. *Her* dark lips plump with huckleberry stain. Enemy as beautiful as Rabbit .. was. *She* has the face of a gentle Bawitčhuwa.

What makes me look close and closer is not beauty but voice.
Words I thought gone are stuck in me .. *She* speaks the language
of White Man.

I force my hands down and try to sit up.

I want to help you, *She* says. Enemy hands flutter flutter around
my face .. *She* does not hide *Her* face like Enemy Rider. *She* hides
nothing. *Her* eyes, lit with stickweed juice and moth wing, shimmer like a green lizard's eyelid.

|He is man| only. And |He is woman| only. How can this be?

I fear this being is *Coyote*.

|He is man|He is woman| is not like Daaża Too Late who
tended cookfires on Hunts.

Daaża Too Late was as mean as sting weed. *S*he watched over Men
and hissed at Women when they walked too close to her Lodge. Daaża
Too Late liked to throw rocks at girls. On thin-Moon nights when Sick
came, *s*he made clay tea from poison root and white-spray carrots, and
instead of killing, *s*he made the Dead come back to living. When Daaża
Too Late wanted Men to return from the Hunt *s*he would go down
to River and scrub white-spray carrots, and rain would come so hard,
Water would run down Mountains, and Men would follow.

|He is woman| is *Coyote* who killed old Woman and emptied
her bowels so *He* could climb inside and become Woman.

When |He is woman| covers me with warm robes I shake and
shake but cannot sh-shake enough to warm myself. I have lost wind.

I feel Water again on my arm tap .. tap ..

Tick la, *She* says to me. Tick la. *She* pats my bound wrists and
ankles, pats *Her* own chest, both sides of *Her* face, shakes *Her* head.
|He is woman| is crying.

I do not believe this Trickster.

Weta lowers her head and grunts.

Days of I have been

with these men all the Seasons of my Life. I have ridden sacked over saddle, my belly pinched of air. In this night so black we sleep blind.

Enemy cinch us to Trees when they stop to sleep. Now I hear and feel Tree blood-sap and gurgle up my spine. On cold nights, Trees nod down their branches and close around us. I feel them breathe out .. and puff .. Life to me.

Wind has changed. Lodge Trees surround us and grass is scruff. We are closer to River. Scents of sour berries and Sweetgrass come. The Earth is colder and dust settles at night.

I am awakened by sounds of rustling.

I blink until I see Stars.

I want to rub my face. I want to turn over. My ankles are swollen in my leggings and I am shivering. I have kicked the robe away.

No crack of fire. No sound of sleep .. If I did not know I would believe I am here alone far from my People. Forever far from Agai River, and from Agai who save me, I am pitiful in my gut.

I pray to my Relations. Smoked Lodge, my Appe, be with me I pray. Do no leave me.

I smell berry shit and bone rot, oil grass of Fish and flies.

I look to see if *Weta* is sleeping. I look fiercely when Moon lists and smolder scarfs Stars. I wait for wind to roll and Sky to clear again.

I hear *Weta* .. moving through grasses .. through smoke brush and thistle. She is slow and fast like a low wind moves grass.

She paws at the ground. She paws at the roots of trees beside me. She snuffles.

I hear her clatter-bang teeth, the slurrupy tongue stir of her mouth. She is close. I smell her. Her hunger smells like wet meat. She rumbles Tree roots and Earth shakes beneath me. Her blackness falls over me and I catch the glint of one oily eye. The Fish of her.

Weta's breath huffs at my ear. My blood beat sounds.

Sniff .. Sniff .. Sniff ..

My ear curls like drying Yampah root.

Has she come to take me?

Long drool glitters from her mouth like Water, like thick spider-thread. She licks the gleam of her paw. Her paw is soggy Earth and black arrow claws.

I do not move. I stay as still as Mouse before the Hawk swipe.

Straggle roots and brush give way as *Weta* stands. Sniffs .. Sniffs.

She is larger than any *Weta* I have seen. Larger than White Weta who clawed No Bear Is His Enemy. Her ears bow forward. Twitch.

In the stillness Enemy Rider slither-sneaks among trees. In wither grasses, I hear his want. His panting.

Weta ruffles and shakes dust-cloud spatter. Pine needles rain from her coat. And then she is gone.

Appe said, You only see Weta when she wants you to see her. I lower my head and slit my eyes but there is only shadows, no scent of Weta, no wood crack.

Enemy Rider taps my foot. The glint of his smile makes my belly shake. He stands to disrobe. He will file me like I am bone. Enemy Rider shoves his breechclout in my mouth and throws himself on top of me.

I buck against Tree. I hold my legs together.

Out of darkness, *Weta* opens her mouth and her mouth is deeper than Sky, darker than the darkness inside her fatty chest. Her arrow-sharp teeth spark close to Enemy Rider.

Enemy Rider yips and runs so fast from me grass lassos his ankles and he falls, and then falls again. He is small in his nakedness and piss fear.

Earth flinches as *Weta* bounces down on all fours to return to her place in Foxtail grass.

Weta harumphs down in her grass nest and licks her big teeth.

Night comes with fester and I become

Spirit. nümukua .. .

Onion Wife rubs her hands together and curls inward. Water dribbles from her mouth over flames and breath-steam rises as Onion Wife rises to tell her story. Bia pulls me close.

Because men, our men, killed White Crow I call out to *must-not-be-named* to show us what is to come .. My heart is a coiled snake. Breath from my broken breast calls up *Weta* from the bones of our stolen Sisters.

Onion Wife circles. Fire cracks and sizzles and Bia pulls me closer and shelters me.

Wronged Mother's sorrow rile the splinter bones of Daughters, and calls Spite, Onion Wife goes on. Her voice pitches like Song.

I call *Weta* to our Lodges. A *Weta* made from palm slaps, bowel growls, dead Women scalps. *Her* coat clacks with the bones of our Dead Daughters. *B*one hair whistling with fire and teeth click. Click .. Chatter .. Click .. When *She* paws Earth, flames rise. Soon the lit Moon will scorch when Earth catches fire.

All their lives, and into on, may War Men pay for what they did to my White Crow.

Bia taps my arm. That does not sound so good, she says. We all suffer and will suffer again.

All the Women quiet. Someone is moving, Buffalo or Bear, down in the feather grass close to River, down low where wind gutters at night, and speaks in the voices of *Spirits*.

It is *Weta*, Onion Wife whispers.

To speak of *must-not-be-named* is to call trouble, Bia says, her breath hot in my ear. A small whirlwind sends twigs and leaves into fire and fire roars.

Click click Click click Click. Teeth spark small lights near River. Do you hear it? Pop Pank asks me.

There on the ground, there on the ground All Around.

Weta is with us now, Onion Wife says.

Do you see Weta, my Baide? Bia asks.

I curl my feet up beneath my robe. Bia does not see what I see. Onion Wife sees. Pop Pank sees *Weta* called from the fizzing lungs of White Crow.

Onion Wife raises her arms and speaks through gurgles of Water. Boom-puff clouds break over us, and Little Moon whimpers. A White Tail breaks through brush and leaps toward us, then away, and Women shoulder together.

Their boats will scrape our River banks, Onion Wife tells us. White Men, the color of teeth, travel toward us. Toward all People. Toward every Tribe. They are War Men, not our own, and without Women will scavenge our unspoken places. Up River they come. Up River they travel.

Their boom-puff *Thunder* and *Spirit-Lightning* will kill us, Onion Wife shouts.

And then low, like a rumble of Buffalo, like a storm of all animals Death will come. Death will come, Onion Wife hisses again. If we must pay with our Daughters, than All will pay.

Her eyes roll. Her tongue trills, Li-li-li-li-li-li-li

The story fire smolders and Smudges Sky . .

What does this mean? I ask Bia.

It means, Never call to *must-not-be-named*. Puh.

Day of Enemy lasts

We climb steep bluffs where Horses only bound up UP and then slide down. Beaded-rock streams trail us to the bottom draw. Enemy Rider clicks his tongue. And Horse tries again and again to climb what cannot be climbed.

Horse leap-kicks and I slide into Enemy's groin.

Enemy pulls me to him so tightly my ribs click.

I bend into a tight half-circle but cannot stop bobbing. I am like a Tree across River quakes.

Horse ki-ki-cks gray dust plumes, s-st-tumbles   *w*-o-b-bles refuses to

cannot *catch*

Earth

becoming clouds.

Horse's back becomes bone slick. And as Horse leap-climbs I feel the ferocious heat of Horse's struggle. Horse's ribs, beneath my own belly, grow with bloat. Slather heat. Foam.

Horse jump-huffs to make up ground and I smell Horse blood scare.

Enemy Rider slip-s, catches my hair. His fingers grasp me. His hands as frantic as Weta's claws snagging Fish. He tears my scalp to hold on.

Enemy Horse rears and I gather all myself to kick off sideways. I fall like rockslides, *pebbles and Earth and me pebbles and Earth and me pebbles.* I roll down and down to end_____ day and feel the scatter of myself, the broken of me. But I am far from Enemy Rider. I am so far from Enemy Rider I can watch him without clamping myself closed.

He flap-kicks his Horse on the crumbling shelf of Earth and Horse jerks up. Kicks. Jerks up. Kicks.

Without warning, neck-straining Enemy Horse springs like a scared Antelope and charges up the crumbly side of the bluff. Up up Up with or without Enemy Rider and Enemy Rider holds on tighter than baby suck--until he cannot. He tumbles off his buck Horse and rolls toward me in a spew of dust. Enemy Rider does not look at me. He dog pants as he scrambles back up the bluff, so steep, so high over our heads Sky quivers.

I slow. Furor rises around me. High Trees bend. Curly-hair grasses wave. When I look up my gut flares. Enemy Rider is going to come to a good bad end. I hold what I see like a good day. I hold what I see like a full basket of berries. I see .. I see .. I see .. I see .. Enemy Horse rears toward Enemy at full strike .. Hooves ignite Captor's head and his bones rattle like stones in a bowl. His blood lights the Sky. A seedpod scattered. A spike-flower.

A *dandelion* .. blown.

Enemy Rider puffs blood as he rolls down and down leaving his blood trail on rocks, on bluff weed.

Dust

settles

and settles.

Done.

Whole of Enemy circles this half-headed Warrior. Horses skitter and flinch in the hoof-clattering commotion of Men sitting or dismounting.

These pitiful Men do nothing but look.

Enemy Rider snorts blood strings.

My bones feel the rock weight of my fall. I am not dead. I am not sacked beside Enemy Rider. I am free. Enemy Rider is cattered meat, a lump of broken. My heart whoops. Enemy Rider cannot come to me. He cannot open me or crack me like Prairie Bird ribs.

|He is man| rides out from the *crow flight* flock of men and their wounded mouth gaping. *He* is the one all Enemy look to.

Cover him in rocks, I yell. Leave him.

Another Enemy strikes me. His hand skitters over my eyes.

My head feels loose, ribs cracked, marrow sucked dry.

Overhead blue grows black. Clouds turn .. drip of dust .. dab of blood .. dribble of baby's milk .. Sky cave of Bears ..

Weta

Weta

Days without

Enemy Men pray in a circle.

|He is man| holds Pipe to the East and hauls then hurls a great wind from *His* lungs and causes smoke to rise from fields. *His Spirit Smoke* becomes a heavy nümü pahamittsi bleeding through Trees.

Lost His Head to Horse lies still. His chest shines toward Stars. His broken head twinkles with crazy gopher eyes. Something swirls from him I do not recognize. Steam buzzes like flies from his dying head.

If I did not despise him, I would pray. Men who return from War do not hate the Enemy.   Now I know why.

They become One.

Women do not become their Enemy captors. We survive them.

Enemy Rider has lost. Old arrow scars have seared his skin the color of spring Camas. His bright scars glow in the tattered smolder-light. The older arrow scars become, the tighter their grip around flesh. I am happy he suffered in battle. Arrow scars cinch flesh as tight as gut string.

Fire rings out dies smolders red.

|He is man| shudders when *He* lifts *His* arms. As *He* changes Nature, light beats and comes together with the high buzz sound of Painan. Trees thrum. A ruckus of bees.

|He is woman| stands before us.

White Man taught me to say *bees*. Bees, He whispered in my ear. *Bees* sound like the thing itself—beez beez beez, He said. Now I hear bees like a whirlwind moving. Painan.

I reach for a rock to help me stand, a branch. I push against Tree and Lightning pain jabs my hip. I catch myself. One leg is weak but I am strong enough to lift myself, to hop.

I see Taken Relations side by side, not tethered, shaking together, holding each other, too afraid to move.

Enemy War Men have gathered around Enemy Rider, their mean faces stopped like a mouse before Owl swoops, like a Deer bowing before camp dogs. Many Claps stands quiet. Pats His Horse twitches. His spanked sad face makes me brave. Wounded Enemy can no longer bolder me.

I yank at my tether. I call my Appe's Mukuapi+n to snake through the legs of my Enemy and capture what is left of Lost His Head to Horse.

Lost His Head to Horse, I shout.

Enemy does not turn from their task.

I buck. I kick. I strain forward to yell. Lost His Head to Horse, I call. Again. Loud. Shaking.

From nowhere, I hear Too Ott Lok. His voice quakes like baby Bird wing flap. Do not speak now, he says.

Puh. Even in Death his *Spirit* is bossy. I am not afraid. Words are big in me. Bigger than frightened. Bigger than Enemy. I spit at their Ceremony.

Be afraid, Lost His Head to Horse. My Appe comes for you, I shout.

I feel shiver over me. Lost His Head to Horse teeters on the edges-of-dark and he is so mean his *Mugua* could return. I am not wrong. Enemy Rider groans.

He is leaving, Too Ott Lok says. Is he tethered beside me? Is Too Ott Lok near?

Sky is the color of Water falls.

Too Ott Lok, I call. Animals rustle near Trees as quiet as grass-hoppers ticking in fields.

Enemy Rider cannot be alive. And Too Ott Lok *is dead* .. I saw him .. unmoving. Fly-eyed.

Am I in the Land of Dzō'apnee?

|He is man| changes again. *His* body stands taller, shifts into War Man. No longer Woman, only Man. I spy no Woman trace, no small, no softness. No berry-stained lips. *He* is strong and wide-shouldered. *His* War scars are small nicks like Stars over *His* body. A thousand arrows never pieced *His* flesh. Never harmed *Him*. Where has the Woman of *Him* gone? *He* is a powerful Enemy. *Shapeshifter. Star* rattler.

Transformation.

His Medicine flares up .. rattle bones of animals.
Rattler tails.
Beavertails slapping hard ground.
Cattail sparkle smoke.
I have never seen such strange power. It rises from *Him* like heat.

|He is man|He is woman| is more than Others. Now |He is Many|.

|He is now Many| gestures to Many Claps Enemy, who races toward me and throws a blanket over my head. Many Claps Enemy wraps my head so tightly I breathe my long-ago self.

Day of Enemy curses

Enemy gathers supplies.

I listen for voices of Toyapi, Keeps Lost Horse, Knife Grass, Gwaču, Traders Daughter.

I read Enemy movements: slivering straps retied on Enemy Horses, Water hiss on fire, *Spirit Bundle's* muffle talk, Enemy Fire Starter's Horse whinnies and bucks.

I remember and know. When Traders Daughter is put on or taken off Enemy Horse her teeth chatter. Enemy coos to her, clucks his tongue. Toyapi whimpers when he is tossed onto Enemy Horse at every day start.

One I name Many Claps claps his hands when he wants to go, now claps his hands.

Pats His Horse pats his Horse three times when ready, now pats his Horse.

|He is woman| rattles sticks in *Her* rock pot and scrapes *Her* cook knife on stones.

Enemy Who Shits grunts at the edge of camp before we go, grunts now. Grunts again. His gut stink fouls every one, everything, every morning, He smears his ass with leaf rubs. I have seen him use whole bushes to clean himself. If he were Agaidika, Men would tease him.

I have not heard Keeps Lost Horse, Knife Grass, or Gwaču.

Where is Otter Woman? I press my hands to Earth and stand. Otter Woman, I call. Weak. Shaking. Blind.

No one answers.

Too Ott Lok speaks again but I do not believe this voice.

She is here with us, the voice says. She is sleeping. Be quiet. Be quiet so we can survive.

Am I tricked by a *bad Spirit*? I listen for the sound only Dead make as they tie Enemy Rider's body to his Horse. Enemy Rider's body makes a sound like gut air whooshing through Night Bird throats.

Hooves patter paw scrape morning ground.

Someone is crying, I lean forward to shake Enemy's wrap. I pull and bite my head covering.

I am lifted and bundled in more blankets. Sacked up. Thrown on Horse sideways, again. Horse lungs wheeze beneath my heart. Horse jostles hops chustles.

|He is woman| speaks but does not remove my head covering. *Her* voice quiet beside me. We are coming to the end of our journey, Little Storm. *She* pets my foot. I wish I could prepare you for what's ahead . . Beauty. Wonder. Unbearable changes. Suffering. Men who wish only for power. White Men who pretend they have power to give. Terrible unforgivables.

I listen with my heart. I listen with my head. I listen with the part of me dying.

I know you hear me, *She* says, and what's more, I know you understand.

I pretend I do not hear but *She* goes on talking.

You no longer need be afraid. We will not hurt you. The Man you call Enemy Rider is half himself. We will take only his good *Spirit* and leave his *bad Spirit* here.

When you pass this way again, and you will, be careful Little Storm. Remember what I am telling you. The *bad Spirit* of the Man who captured you will haunt this place. Do not be alone here. Do not go off from others.

I want to ask how |He is woman| knows these things but know *Her* medicine is not to be spoken.

I hear the crack of *Her* smile. Oh, *She* says, and beware of Corn Women, *She* whispers, They will eat you.

Days breaks

over great and vast and open grasses. I hear low Land's red Song. Wind rustles and tugs, yellow then white, and grasses return the old Songs.

Many Women gather. They whisper together in grasses when they do not wish their Husbands to know what they do. I know their Song warnings. I listen. My feet tethered. I am in a Land no longer my own. The scents around me are not scents I know. My legs jolt and stiffen out like a butchered Deer. My body is broken. My body is a different Country. A different River breaks my blood. *Weta* roars ..

Roars over my hush liver.

Roars over my sleep hands.

Roars into days no longer me.

Roars into gone .. Appe   Bia   Cameahwait   Blue Elk   Otter Woman   Pop Pank.

His roar becomes voices of Rivers, patters of Water. Sparkling hands of Ogres.

When I breathe out, no more,

No more

no me.

Enemy unravels Elk-wrap. My head steams. Snow scatters over Land All Around. Fog. Cold.

How long have I been covered? How long have I been gone?

Slowly light. Slowly scent. Slowly stone   mint   Men—*Spirit*-sick wanderers. Before us wide grasslands seedy with animals. Behind us, the dim shade of forests.

At the edges-of-dark Lost His Head to Horse rides Enemy Horse round and round Trees. More shadow than Man. More gone than here. His head a jagged cliff. His eyes as flat as whittle rocks.

Enemy Who Shits ties Lost His Head to Horse behind Enemy
Horses and leads him out.

|He is now Many| stands before Moon, stands above grassland-
into-forever. I hear with the ears of all my Relations. On these
Plains—Buffalo are born, their great mewling skitters over the vast
Lands like sharp hooves. Rabbit hearts beat in wind-woven grasses.
Coyotes snigger along River edge.

|He is now Many| pulls *Spirit Bundle* off *His* Horse. *He* unlaces
the opening and lifts *It* above *His* head.
|He is now Many| shakes *Bundle* to awaken *Its* power.
Bundle is quiet. Unlaced. Open to us all.
Antelope legs kick out at Enemy.
Enemy Fools have captured, and now unleash, a Monster
from sluver Water. Mist rises—swish breaths—Water sprays from
Bundle's pouch-mouth. Mushroom smell coils.
Spirit Bundle births a Water Baby with straggle hair.
Water Baby shakes and shakes.
When Water Baby spits at Enemy, they laugh. A voice as frail
as Bird shell croaks from rib-winged Water Baby. I know the voice.
Enemy has captured .. Pop Pank.
Pop Pank. Pop Pank. My Sister. Pop Pank, I call.
My head is sacked again.

Day of Burial hive

Fires crackle. Sparks.

We have come to our stop place. I hear crying. All Around. A Man gathers me like a slack pouch. Carries me. Uncovers my face.

Round dirt walls circle us—a large Prairie Dog Lodge—a giant hive.

Enemy Warriors have left us. Gone is |He is man|He is woman| He is now Many|, Pats His Horse, Berry Eater, Horse Leader, Lost His Head to Horse. All gone but Enemy Who Shits.

We have come to the place inhabited by the *ghosts* of my Taken Relations. We are not ourselves here. We are only shimmer of self. Sky dances with the blood of my Appe. His scalp hair twists in the wind over my Captor's Lodge.

Otter Woman stands in shadows, her dusty hair matted like Buffalo shoulders, her eyes scorched. I squint to see a thin boy. Too Ott Lok? He lifts his hand to me as sleepy as when he suckled his Bia's teat. Pop Pank shivers, so sick she will not survive three days. I reach for them. I shout their names. We struggle to touch hands. To come together.

Man with silt-color hair carries Pop Pank screaming from us. I hear her far away and moving farther from me. The sound of her voice quakes in my chest.

Otter Woman, thin as a cattail, signs to me, We live on like Running Woman.

My ribs ache without fat, without Bia, without Blue Elk. If Enemy were to gut me they would find only teeth, bubbled bones, lungs as watery as Rivers.

Where have they taken Toyapi, Keeps Lost Horse, Knife Grass, Gwaću, Traders Daughter?

They buried Traders Daughter, Otter Woman signs. She is gone.

I am too weak to tell, my Sister, Blue Elk comes for us. In Earth Lodge, Running Women are not-be-afraid.

Day of gone Too Ott Lok

White Men swarm the great Earth Lodges carrying pelts, glittering worthless things. In and out, in and out. They are pack rats. Head-stormed and hectic. They cannot get enough of everything.

Appe's voice chuffs in my ear. Listen. Learn.

White Man taps my forehead. Commit these words to memory. Pay attention.

I learn their ways. They bring in their Beaver skins and piles of furs and trinkets. White Men spread their things and point. Count them, one White Man says. Count.

While we sleep with full bellies, they carry Too Ott Lok away from us like Buffalo hide.

Too Ott Lok, Otter Woman cries. He is pitiful. He will not live without his Bia. Pop Pank is strong. She can outlive any man. Any creature. All these Monsters.

We must live for our Taken Relations, I tell Otter Woman.

Poor poor Too Ott Lok, she cries again.

Look at how broken we have become, I tell her. We care for Too Ott Lok when our own lives are weak? We did not care for Too Ott Lok when we were strong. We left him behind like animal droppings. Like oily berry plop.

Otter Woman is quiet for a long time. Struck. Frozen Deer meat.

I have said too much. Appe told me I was not mean when I left Too Ott Lok. Now I feel mean as Badger, mean as old gut stink. Mean as survival is mean. Mean as Coyote. Mean is not good Relations.

Otter Woman drops her head. Her look gouges me. I have betrayed our Old Ways.

A low sound comes from her throat. A low sound like the deepest sad. I rub her shaking back. And then I understand . . Otter Woman is laughing. She laughs and laughs and Enemy eyes us like gopher holes.

Day of gamble voices

You live here now, they tell us through sign. A'aninin, they say, hitting their proud chests. I collect their signals. They are the People of the White Clay. I listen. I learn new words every day.

A'aninin, I say.

A'aninin feed us dried orange rounds, soft pebble beans. Our bellies bloat. We shit yellow.

They bring back Pop Pank. I cry to see her. My eyes Wolf her small self. If Pop Pank is good, I am good.

Do not be quick, Otter Woman says. She was brought back for bad purpose.

We have been here for many days, trapped inside with Horses, Enemies, and White Men. I hear sounds of Many outside. Women gaddering. Men whooping. Children playing games. Clops of running Horses. People, plentiful as mice, talk day and night. So many different talk ways. I hear splinters of White Men words. A few White Men Geese honks. Men who talk through their nose.

Quand le jeu commencera-t-il? frazzle-gruff White Man says.

Shouts and Songs travel to us from River. Drum Songs.

We are surrounded by Watchers, their eyes like the beads of tiny Bird eyes—pebbled eyes.

They see see see, not us. I am sick with their eyes, I say.

Eyes are easy to trick, Pop Pank says. You will see, she jokes.

Men arrive with snow on their shoulders. Cold snakes round the Lodge like bitter breath. Water Babies shriek as River slows. We huddle close and closer. And the Men count and count and count. One hundred, they say. One hundred and one. One hundred and two. On and on. The same words over and over.

Otter Woman's eyes speckle in firelight. Do you hear them? she whispers.

I listen.

I hear Bia in the hard lament of frozen Water. *My Baide,* she says, *Why do you not mourn me?*

We grow stronger. They feed us Buffalo and dried berries, orange rounds cooked in clay bowls. Men eye us like fat Horses.

Enemy Who Shits tosses a small hide pouch into circle of White Men. He points at me and then at Otter Woman. I see bones in the hands of players.

Lost His Head to Horse spins in and out of firelight and laughs to himself. His broken head grown over, healed without healing. Here and there his raggedy half-skull is spiky. A porcupine roach of bone. When he squats beside me I see his heart beat in the soft bowl of his head . . Otter Woman stands and hisses him away. She butts him with her chest when he tries to touch me and he crumples. He moves away from Otter Woman but cannot be chased away. He stands behind gamblers with a half-smile and points at me and then at himself.

She is a good one, White Men say, pointing at Otter Woman. If you are lucky, you will win her. But that little one, a squint Man says, nodding toward me, She is not old enough to make babies. If she's nine years old I'll eat my Horse.

The old White Man, Nagutah—the One-who-honks—grunts when he eyes me. Licks his thin lips.

Charbonneau likes them young, the squint Man says. He likes flat chests, tight trapcheeks. He likes to break young girls.

When Otter Woman asks what they are saying, I tell her I do not know.

Men whistle and blow their breaths into gamble throws. Men hide bones and flash their big chomp teeth.

Nothing
        No One
                No Animal skin
                No Horse
                        No Woman
                        No Child
                                Is safe from their owning games.

Bone click
        Bone click
                Bone click.

Days of Knife River

Now. I am cut from my People.

I am no one Here. I am Gambled away. I am worth less than an animal pelt of one.

Poked by Men. Lifted and thumped like cattered meat for scraps.

We have been won by Nagutah, White Man Goose. Charbonneau they call him.

Pop Pank has been taken by a Woman and Man. I no longer hear her screams.

Charbonneau huffs at other gamblers and preens as he gathers us up.

When Old Goose leads us outside we shake from cold. He wears Buffalo robes.

We wear blood pong and capture wounds.

He offers us nothing. No Water. No fire. No skins.

Metaharta, he says to us.

Charbonneau takes us to his Lodge. His Lodge is not big but it is fat with his belongings. From circle poles hang Rattle tails and Snake skins and Beaver pelts and little Rabbit's feet the color of Sky. We stare at cook bowls the color of bee spit and shining light, hung from a broken Tree branch.

He must cook for *Spirits*, Otter Woman says.

Day of Otter Woman

Charbonneau squats. Dangles his broke-sack balls down down ..
into my face and I swat away his stench, his unbearable body sick.
Curdled teat. Rancid smoke oil. Wither bone. Death.

Man-who-plagues-us, Otter Woman says, if you touch this girl
before she bleeds as Woman, you will sleep alone with your throat
cut. She is too young. Look at her. She is a baby.

I am nine summers old though my Womb has been split by
Enemy Captor.

If you touch my Sister, Otter Woman tells Man-who-plagues-us
over and over, I will Badger you. I will claw your eyes out. I will slit
your ball sack and toss them to black Birds.

Man-who-plagues-us does not understand Otter Woman's
words. He understands the spit-glare of her eyes.

When Otter Woman and I are alone we cut our hair and slash
our legs with a knife stolen from Man-who-plagues us. I cut my hair
close to my scalp for all my gone Relations.

Bia, I mourn you.

Appe, stay near me.

Man-who-plagues-us returns and slaps his chest, and mine. Tu
ressembles à un garçon, he says.

He is too stupid to know Blue Elk comes for me. Blue Elk's
arrival chuffs behind us like fire wind. Blue Elk will tear this Enemy
from mouth to cock, leaving nothing but Crow bones .. pale
shine ..

Day of no-good work

Man-who-plagues-us leaves after his long rasp sleep. He does not rise like Hunter. He would sleep all day if he did not wake to our work. He takes Beavers we have skinned and returns with more Beavers to skin, skinny Deer to butcher, pockets heavy with Rabbits. But he is lazy. Not great Hunter. He haunches around us while we gather green and dry willows for smolder fires. His eyes sticky on us. He believes we will bound for the hills, leap from him like Antelope.

We boil Water in his shiny orange kettles, soak hides, and then roll hides in ashes, and scrape. He watches us while we work, squints through smoke, and turns the tanning skins and sniffs them. We stand all day in smoke fires until our skin turns dull.

Otter Woman says we will become as yellow as his buckskin.

He signs to us, This is mine and this is mine and this is mine. We stir sting weed into his Rabbit stew. We laugh. He owns every small thing, Otter Woman says. Every berry seed and fat drip.

His sting-green shit is his, I say, and we laugh more.

I make a wooden knife I sharpen on hot stones until it slices gristle like melt fat. He sneers at my work and at my knife. When Charbonneau is watching I slice through a muscly Deer haunch in one cut and hack the bone to pieces.

Beaver fur shines around us, so many more hang from every pole in his Lodge. When Charbonneau is near, we keep our eyes down. When he is away we walk through the Village looking for Too Ott Lok and Pop Pank. We are close to other Lodges and hear families and laughing children, watch Women who smile and grind Corn.

A'aninin Women squint at us behind cook-fire smoke. Sneak looks from their Lodge doors before we are invited inside. We cannot be trusted. They have seen stolen Sisters before. In the brittle cold days of our capture their breath puffs clouds. Peck talk peck peck peck.

They offer us food but watch us like we are Wolverines, like we have come to take what is theirs. Their Lodges are so big their Horses are tethered inside. We watch them together and go back to the Lodge of Man-who-plagues-us. Nothing is here for us but work. Why does the White Man want so many Beavers? Beavers speak to me. I hear the Song of their Deaths.

Hear me, my Relation, I whisper to Beaver. If you give us back Pop Pank and Too Ott Lok we will give offerings to your family.

Otter Woman watches.

We listen. We wait.

Days of Enemy strut

When Charbonneau walks us through Mandan Village he struts like War Man with many scalps. Mandan is filled with White Men, Indian traders, travelers. I have never seen so much commotion, so many People. They jostle and ride Horses for show. Children play foot games and Women tend to Lodges. Everywhere there are kettle fires and talk and work. A good smell of smoke and sizzle fat, Beaver jerky and roots. People look at Charbonneau, bob their shoulders, hiss. Man-who-plagues-us does not see their laughs. He sees his watery bloat-face looking back at his self. He is blind to his own trickery.

We see a great Lodge with many colors and long scarves. We smell Sweetgrass and Sage

Berdache, Charbonneau says. He lifts his scraggly eyebrow to us, and then he moves far ahead of us again.

Charbonneau has us walk Lodges behind him. He holds our shoulders and makes us stay like dogs if we walk beside him. He does not look to see if we keep up. He does not see me snagged by tall Woman. Otter Woman is busy with what she sees. She does not see I am not with her.

Little Storm, the Woman says. She pulls off her hood and *She* is |He is woman|. *She* chatters like fast Water. White Man words click and hiss.

I'm sorry, *She* says. I talk too fast. *She* slows *Her* talk and signs to me. *She* moves and the shells on *Her* arms jickle.

I .. am .. sorry. Little Storm. *She* touches my shoulder. Jickle.

All other sounds halt and shimmer around me like Hummingbird wings. The whole Village gadder. All commotion. All People talk. I hear only *Her*. I do not know all *Her* words but words come back to me. *Remember, White Man said. Re-mem-ber.*

I remember Little. Storm. I remember Sorry. I remember White Man. *I'm sorry I follow you. You must be tired of me.*

I'm sorry you were gambled away, *She* signs, and says, and to him, of all People. |He is woman| looks up.

To him .. of .. all People, I say. I do not see what *She* says. *I do not know, White Man said. I do not know how to teach you.*

It comes to me. I do not *know what She* says. *Her* face glitters like Debai-lit River.

Oh, damn, *She* says. Here he comes. I will find you. Jickle jickle. We will talk. I will teach you.

Teach me? |He is woman| will teach me?

I am like sweet smoke rising with blessings. I am hollow and light as Milkweed. I do not look at Charbonneau. I turn from him. I look All Around like I am blind but I am blind to him alone.

He kicks me in the buttocks but he does not hurt me. He cannot hurt me now. I do not fall.

Charbonneau does not see |He is woman| because he cannot see.

He makes Otter Woman and I walk behind him, closer, but still back from him.

Who were you talking to? Otter Woman asks.

Beautiful Enemy, I answer, and hear .. my heart ..

At his Lodge, Charbonneau clangs and sharpens his axe. When I nest down for sleep he grabs me, and Otter Woman stops him. She stops him from me.

Otter Woman will not wash her Woman hole. She smells like curdled Fish. String-gut kettles. Forgotten Fish eggs.

Man-who-plagues-us sucks her teat but will not mount her.

Oof, he says, Oof when he pulls up her robe.

When he falls asleep, Otter Woman pats my arm and covers her mouth to keep from laughing.

Our names for Charbonneau are plenty. Man-who-plagues-us, Old Goose, Old Gruff, Old Grope, Long Sack, Oily Eyes, Slippery Man, Tinder Teeth, Snigger, Oof.

For Capture Women, names are survival. Not to bathe is survival. We have names for all ways Charbonneau is, all ways Metaharta changes, all clacks and stubbles and shouts. All quiet and noise. Any animal moves near or away. Any snake slither. Any mouse scratch. Small noises are large in us. We know when to run, when to stop like stones.

Charbonneau travels up River, alone, but all along tracks us. We brush our steps with stick bundles, hide what we gather. We look to our work when he sniffs our baskets and caches. He hides his berries and roots from us, and slaps our hands to keep us from his Rabbit kettles filled with sage and Juniper. He is wise to us. He knows we will poison him by little bits. We Fish out his tender Rabbit bites. Find his dried sweet cherry baskets buried beneath his many robes.

Children walk past us like tight-footed Coyotes—watchful of Tinder Teeth's snap—but we have ways to survive.

Days of All Ways to survive

Food is plentiful here but I track Bird scratch and eat seeds.

You are skinny as Hidatsa Horse, Otter Woman tells me. What are you doing digging around snow like Rabbit? Eat. Stingy Oof will make you eat Tree bark.

Otter Woman eats and eats. She eats beans and squash and pumpkin. She eats Buffalo and Mountain Goat. She has become as plump as fat plums. Her thighs swish-swish.

She has forgotten when you are thin, you can run fast. You can hide behind saplings. You can run from your Enemies.

I track One Eye as he moves in and out of Trees and peeks in and out of Lodges. He makes no sound. He shadows the People and stalks Women like Cougar. Men thin as reeds weave through Trees and River willows, looking here, looking there. Watchers. Men who wear no moccasins, no covering to shield them. It is so cold their nakedness smokes.

I hold my breath and steady my watch. If I do not keep steady I cannot see them. They shimmy up Trees. They snake River rocks. If they know I spot them, they fade away like Weta. When One Eye stands alone, his presence is taller than Elk shoulder. He is ribby in his nakedness, and moves like always stalking animals, quiet, without sound. His one eye sharp as a lance.

I walk where they walk and see no tracks. No sign. They are sneaky Watchers.

Otter Woman is not keen-sighted. She busies her eyes on her work. She does not believe I see naked Men in Trees. What would they want? she asks. Maybe you make up stories because you have no stories to tell. Tend to what is, Otter Woman says, or you will end up crazy in the bushes like your Bia.

She is not wrong. I have been without my People's stories, without Onion Wife and Bia, without Appe, without Agai, without rocks or Ogres who tell their own stories. I know the sound Hills and Mountains make when winter nears. I know reed talk and root Song. I know all sounds of Agai River in All Seasons, and I know their stories. They speak to me.

Here, Land shouts or whistles at night, or changes to what it is not. Gathering becomes sharp Land drops or bone-shatter rocks, sand swirls, mud sucks, and too-close Buffalo. I fear night when wind becomes voices and heaves with sounds of crying, and Death, and whole Villages hover up River rising from whispery dust. Wind shudders beneath Charbonneau's Lodge and swirls around like it is looking. Like it is seeking. Otter Woman does not know that a Woman without her People, a Woman who can never return is crazy. I am crazy with want for Appe and Bia, and Blue Elk, but I am not crazy.

Lost His Head to Horse sees One Eye and his Men too. He looks up when I look up. He tracks them with his eyes and body sway. His crazy ways keep me.

If Lost His Head to Horse did not clash his teeth, I would not know he is everywhere. Stalking me. Watching me. Chomping behind me like Deer in sparse grass. He is like One Eye and his slinky Men. I have learned enough Hidatsa to know what Lost His Head to Horse says.

Lost His Head to Horse shouts, I want you. You will have my babies. You will sing to me alone. I want your puppy teats. He sings to me with his Elk rut calls, with his broken head humming with blood. He sings and sings. A'aninin Women come out of their Lodges to look. White Men traders gawk. Lost His Head to Horse makes me laugh without want. When I tire of him I chase him with a stick.

I ask Lost His Head to Horse who One Eye is. He takes my talk as sign I want him. He jumps like a Fish leaps for flies. Why? He asks, twitching. You want One Eye?

No, I say. Do you want One Eye? I ask to tease. Lost His Head to Horse looks wounded. His eyes sink like rotten plums. He slaps at his face. He jigs his shoulders and turns from me. I see him crouching in tall grasses, beneath berry bushes. He covers his eyes now when he sees me.

You should be happy, Otter Woman tells me, you rid yourself of Lost His Head to Horse. Some days Otter Woman is Bia.

Days pass and Lost His Head to Horse keeps himself from me. I do not see him in the gather bushes, or along River. I do not see his lurk self. He is gone. But when I scrape Beaver hides, there he is like a sneaky-footed Prairie dog. He stands too close because he does not want others to hear, and he cannot whisper with a broken head.

One Eye is Chief, he tells me. He is not like other Chiefs.

Lost His Head to Horse twitches and shakes as he tells me many stories. He tries to keep his voice from rising. One Eye watches All, from Metaharta to Mandan, All White Men, All traders, and All Indians who come to trade. He says, One Eye has many Watchers.

White Men call him Cyclops. You would not want him. No, he shakes his head, and squats. Because you are with me, he says, One Eye would chase you down and chop your head. You would be like me, he says. He killed one wife. He will kill you. He will kill me. After he tells me too many stories, he scritters away.

Why do you speak to him? Otter Woman asks. What can he know? He has lost half his head. We have enough bother here. Now he will leech you.

Otter Woman is not wrong. I carry my digging stick with me. Lost His Head to Horse told me what I need. One Eye is like Appe before Enemy surrounded us. Appe crouching in grasses. Appe hiding in Trees. What Enemy does One Eye wait for? I fear I will not be able to leave under his watch.

One Eye walks two places. The *Spirit* place and here. He and his Watchers are like Small Pox Dead who haunt the empty Villages, who light fires into on. He is the flicker light in grasses.

I make a bowl out of rock. I chisel and scrape and burn bowl smooth. I give my work to Beaver.

I ask Beaver to help. I ask Beaver to take pity on me and on my Taken Relations. I look across River, across thick grease-ice where gut-black Water hides. River skin so thick, ice smokes.

Weta stands and shakes snow from her coat.

For days and days River screeches with cold. Wind roars down over us. Mice skitter through caches. Lodge poles creak. Whirling fires cannot keep away cold. Grasses and Trees fringe with ice.

Antelope and Deer, Elk and Goats and Buffalo rush from Mountains and Plains and shelter in blue-trunked Trees where *Water Spirits* call. All night animals cry. Their scare becomes fog.

Water Spirits wait beneath thin River skin to snatch the pitiful and weak. Whole herds break through ice. I hear their clatter-hooves, their night wails, as River closes around and over them.

Day of Beaver

Charbonneau would not want us to use his axe to chop River ice, so we do. We hack the ice where White traders jig lines for whisker Fish.

A low growl croons over ice.

Did you hear that? I ask.

It is ice, Otter Woman says. See it rubbing against itself? Otter Woman stares down into the ice hole we've chopped, into the deep hole where dark Water gathers.

A small Woman squats on the other side of River. She is hidden in tall basket willows, close to where Beavers hide their food branches, but I see her. The Woman lifts her hand for me to follow and holds her palm up for Otter Woman to stay.

Otter Woman does not stop me. The Woman is dressed in shiny Beaver skins. Old Man Gruff would eye her like trinkets. The Woman's wither smell sneaks over me like whiff of Death rocks and Muskrat burrows. Together, the Woman and I walk step by step over ice-slick mud, over and around suck holes, and sticker bush, and as we walk, her wet hair freezes like bitten saplings, like thin braided Fish weirs.

Do not be afraid of me, she says. When she turns toward River her teeth spark; when she turns toward me her teeth blacken with snag holes. We walk until the bluff overhead grows tall and hides us.

Far above us campfires snap and smoke. I hear the People talk, laugh, work, cook.

She points her chin to a child out on thin River skin. A girl. Beyond the girl black Water shivers. The Woman nods. Wind slivers snow. River sounds click-clacky-click-clacky click click like Crows picking bones.

must-not-be-named looks for you, she says.

I do not ask questions.

This is your answer, she tells me. Ice splinters. River roars, Water swells, and the Woman dives in, and is gone.

But River is not broken. Deep green ice kettles the black River. No ice breaks until Corn breaks Earth. Boys slide and chase each other on River hard as stones.

When I return to camp, Otter Woman sits me by the fire and brings me scalding marrow broth. Where did you go? she asks. I turned and you were not behind me.

Did you not see the Woman? I ask. She pats my hand and pulls her blanket off to wrap around me.

It is so cold campfire smoke rises straight into stars.

All night I hear Beaver tails slap snow to ice. I feel the heat from slapping tails as they pass around Charbonneau's Lodge. Lodge poles shake with each tail slap.

Do you hear our Relation? I ask Otter Woman.

I hear someone running outside Lodge, Otter Woman says. They must be heavy. Whole Earth Lodge shakes.

Wurtle-eyed Charbonneau takes his gun and steps out. He finds nothing but butt fall.

When Debai leaks through the Lodge, Otter Woman shows me the ice circle Beaver made All Around Charbonneau's Lodge.

Days of Birds wake Water

A hundred Birds, and a hundred Birds more, clot in Tree beside River and wait. Tree jitters with flittery Birds, and more, and more flittery Birds. And then, up together as One, Tree to Tree, branch to branch, fluttering together, pulling together, churning wind, they wake winter-sleeping River.

Ice moans. Ogres chant. And shot gun .. River runs.

We back from the slosh and roar, the clatter and bang of River moving.

All things work together, Appe told me. In Freezing Season, Fish, Frogs, Eels call Birds to move Rivers. Birds wake the Earth.

And buffalo come. Buffalo bobbing in Water. Bubbling. Fizzing. A herd so many in number, so swollen by their own gasses, they look as light as puff clouds. Buffalo burble and bounce, clog River bends. Men ready their poles, and as the bloated Buffalo near, they spear them. Sour Buffalo gut steams green.

River booms and more ice and Buffalo floats come. The People run through the Village shouting.

Look. See, I tell Otter Woman. River is free.

Thick ice-jags careen past, and Men jump on and pole and jostle toward Buffalo. Whole Tree jams break from ice, their roots waggle, wobble, slam River bank. Men pole and push Trees aside and onward.

A Woman jumps from ice cake to ice cake as River ice bumps around her.

Where did all these People come from? Otter Woman asks. I have never seen so Many.

We shelter in willows and watch a Woman line up her knives. We will feast on Buffalo meat that melts like fat over fire, she says, licking her lips.

A family links arms and runs toward River together. A Buffalo stomp of People. White Men stand on the high bluff, arms folded, gape-mouthed. A few White Men gruff among the crowd, startled and lip strung.

I spot Pop Pank running through families, dodging, jumping. Wild-eyed. She is not dressed for cold.

Look, I tell Otter Woman. Pop Pank. Do not let her out of your watch!

I chase after Pop Pank. I duck through People. Pop Pank! I shout. Pop Pank! A Woman pushes past me and a Man stops in front of me. I lose sight of her. I squat to look through legs. I stand on broken wood to make myself tall.

Do you see her? I call to Otter Woman. Otter Woman cups her hands to her eyes. I run back to her. Frantic. But Otter Woman is not watching Pop Pank. I follow her gaze. Her eyes glitter on a tall, slender Man naked to waist. An unbroken arrow pierces his chest, in through one side, stuck out the other. Death-pierced, but alive. His aliveness makes him Only. Alive Beside Arrow steadies himself and walks apart from all People. If he fell he would gouge his self, Dead.

Is he a *Spirit*? Otter Woman asks. Her breath is soft clouds, smoke blown from Sacred pipe.

Li-li-li-li-li-li-li the Women call.

Men jump from ice slab to ice slab to corral Dead Buffalo. Puss-hiss and bile-gas gurgle-leak stink All Around. My eyes water-sting. White Men gasp. Clap. A few White Men empty their bellies onto the steaming snow.

Alive Beside Arrow steps from the ice sheet he rides. He is so close I see the yellow feather arrow sticking out both sides of his middle. His face is delicate and watchful. A dead Man living.

Out from a small group of children Pop Pank runs to River.

Pop Pank, I shout. She runs to where River swirls like angry snakes, a muscly torrent stronger than Buffalo Runs—wider.

I look up to see Pop Pank jump from a rock overhang and re-member her Gagu. She arches her back before she closes on herself.

A Turtle. A shade bug. She hits black Water—-hiss—and Water wardles around her, over her. She pops up like a cut rib bone. Ogre tongues flit between ice and churn Water harder, faster. Giant ice shards crack.

When I reach River, Otter Woman catches the tail end of my robe. No, she says. You cannot follow her.

I fight but Otter Woman holds fast. Near us Broken River claws, shifts, screeches.

Pop Pank's head lifts from furious Water, ducks beneath an ice cake, and then I see her . . no more.

I pull away from Otter Woman but now Charbonneau's hands grip me. Old Man Gruff holds tight when I gouge and scratch him, when I kick and bite him. But when I turn with my raised fists it is not Charbonneau I see, it is Alive Beside Arrow. His eyes are still as a prayer Bird.

The People celebrate their polled catch. Young children fist soft bloated Buffalo meat into their mouths. All night there is singing and dancing.

I wait for Pop Pank and River runs on. Black then green. Green then blue. River stones gurgle and fizz, and Mud Squatter's voice oils River, Moon after changing Moon, into the Season of Heat and Gather.

On dark nights, *Bia* joins me. Many Seasons have passed, *she* says. *She* grips my arm. We sit in the way I sat with Appe, the smoke of our breath lifting to Stars, chickering like winter frost after winter has passed.

Days of surrounded

I smile at the Women at Metaharta. I catch up to them and clean their scrape tools and awls. I help them skin and cook. I sharpen their knives. I learn to speak their language, better than Charbonneau, and they bring me their best duck fat, their heaviest Buffalo tongues.

Charbonneau is happy I work in great fields of Squash and Corn. He does not know I learn his language, too.

To parles trop, he tells me.

Corn fields surround us. Sweet scent of Corn follows me. Sunflowers bow their giant heads over me. I hear their sighs and small witherings. Gold bees fly from them but do not sting me.

You listen to our Sacred Ones, A'aninin Women tell me.

A'aninin Women are beautiful in all their ways. They are tall and hardy. Some have eyes the color of Sunflower seeds. Others have eyes the color of honeyed Corn.

You should see Mandan Corn, A'aninin Women tell me. Corn stalks so big a small one like you would get lost. They tell me about hidden Corn fields where Mandan Women fly like Crows, where Corn grows as high as bluffs, where giant herds of Deer rest in Corn shade, and Corn *Spirits* watch over Corn fields. They speak with ease about *must-not-be-named*. Our gardens in Metaharta and Mandan feed many People. But this garden, bigger than All gardens, is kept hidden. A garden of Sacred Corn Teeth to carry the People into on.

I cannot tell if they tease. Could there be bigger gardens? They share their plenty with me. They show me their ways of basket weaving and gathering. I listen and learn but do not forget I am in Enemy Camp.

I hide in the dark Corn paths away from Otter Woman and Charbonneau. No one knows where I am—no one—but |He is woman|. *She* finds me even when I am far far away in the watery trough of the furthest Corn row. I hear *Her* tiny jingling bells first, and then *Her* clicking beads, and all *Her* clattering clattering bone bangles. The first time *She* found me, *She* frightened me with *Her* mirrors flashing light through the Corn rows.

Look what I brought, *She* said, waving a flutter. It's paper. I can show you words now. I told you I would find you. We sit among the Corn, and letter by letter, word by word, *She* teaches me English.

But when I ask |He is woman|, Why do you bother with me? Why do you give me your time?

Mice skitter.

Corn stalks shift and close around us, and Debai no longer trickles to me.

Rocks click together. Wind sniffles.

Edges-of-dark writhe in and around Corn stalks but do not harm me.

I come into the presence of |He is now Many|.

|He is now Many| tells me, We have always known your story.

|He is now Many| now comes to me more than |He is woman|.

|He is now Many| changes Sky.

He is flooding Waters

sudden rains

clatters of Lightning.

Everything hums in *His* presence.

My deepest insides cocoon and quiet.

His questions stop me. Flitter in me.

What do you understand? What do you think? What do you imagine?

Understand . . *He* says, is to know. You see with your eyes.

He circles *His* hand. All this you see.

Do you know that I see what you see?

Do you also know that although I see what you see, what I see can be different than what you see? Even when we look at the same thing, you see from your eyes. I see from mine.

You do not see your face, I say. And I do not see mine.

He nods. Yes. We understand we see from different eyes. But to truly understand is to know that there is this, and this, between us. *He* swishes the air around us. *He* taps *His* heart. *He* taps mine.

Close your eyes, *He* says. Do you see *me*?

No, I say. My eyes are closed.

But because your eyes are closed, does that mean you cannot see me? You see me.

Yes. I do. I see *you*.

Tell me, Little Storm, where is it that you see me?

In here, I say. In my head.

And because we understand, and know, we can imagine what it is like for each other.

Sometimes you laugh with others. Sometimes you don't. Why? When you begin to ask yourself why, you begin to understand.

What do you think? *He* asks. White Man thinks with his head. Wise People think with their bones, with their sinew. Sit with River and River thinks in you. Do you understand, Little Storm?

Your Appe and your Bia helped you to be aware. Now think with All that is around you. Consider what others think. To consider others is to think for yourself and another.

What do you imagine?

I do not know, I say. What is imagine?

You are a Bird flying over our heads. Can you see it? *He* taps my skull.

Do you *see*? See yourself flying high above us. See over the high tassels of Corn. See over Mountains. Look down and see the lit paths of All the animals. See yourself with your Bia. Can you see, Little Storm?

Yes, I say, I always see Bia.

Yes, |He is now Many| says. Yes. See yourself understanding.

|He is woman| tells me funny stories of Mandan dances. Two Hidatsa Sisters sewed a long robe. The small Sister climbed up on the shoulders of the big Sister, and then they put on the dress they had made. When they walked into the Village they scared the men who had been cruel to them.

She tells me stories about the Villages that once lined River. *She* tells me Buffalo charged a near Village and destroyed everything. Buffalo so fast their hooves caught grasses on fire. Buffalo did not come out of meanness or spite, *She* says. They were running from Death.

She tells the story of Woman-Who-Never-Died.

When I try to retell the story to Otter Woman, I cannot. I cannot remember.

Do not worry, |He is woman| tells me. Stories live in every word.

Days of Debai

Debai lights the Village and *Men-must-not-be-named* pass by Earth Lodges with fire-lit eyes. They are Men, and They are not Men. They are bigger, wider. Sacred. Their bodies painted with vermillion and white clay. They change that which is All Around them.

Debai hovers, sizzles River fog and cloaks the People in clouds. A'aninin Women feel brave now. Debai gives them power. They talk loudly about White Men who bring trade goods and trouble.

Bold A'aninin Women shout at White Men from the doors of their Lodges, Do not swarm us. Go home. You bring nothing but bad Medicine.

They poison our Men with want, they tell me. Now nothing pleases them.

Women point their lips and spit at White Men unloading carry dogs and Horses. They tread our paths and trample good Medicine. They come for us even after our Men give us away to them. They defile our Ceremonies.

The White Men do not step aside as *Men-must-not-be-named* pass. They skunk-twitch and sleep-eye the Sacred.

In Charbonneau's Lodge, Horses skitter and rear . . Wind chases dust, whips and whistles, and shrills. My robe flares and catches me up. I am a Bird flapping. I am small heartbeats in a giant Land.

I become bold. I ask A'aninin Women if they have seen other Shoshoni. Have they seen Too Ott Lok?

They do not answer. They look to their work.

I hear Bia's voice. *Look with your gut, my Baide, then you would have no need for questions.*

I do not listen. I am as strong as Running Woman, I tell A'aninin Women. She is both great Hunter and basket maker. You would remember Her. She could chase White Men away.

Puh, I say like Bia. My chest puffs as I talk, Running Woman does not run as fast as Horses, but She runs their distance.

A'aninin Women sniff and turn from me. But one stays. Corn Necklace brings me gifts of Corn baskets. She listens when I talk. She smiles like I am one of her own but she is only Seasons older.

My face is hot. It is the Season of Sun Dance. It is the Days of thanks and suffering. And the Days of humble. It is not Days to talk big.

Day of sputter talk

Charbonneau says he will take you to People of First Man where he will have you work with Mandan Corn Women. This is his way to scare you.

What is to fear of Women who tend Corn? I talk big again.

Have you not heard stories? Otter Woman asks. She nips sinew thread with her knife and flaps her hand. Charbonneau thinks you will not run from Corn Women. He tells me, who runs from Women who kill Buffalo without weapons? Who runs from Women who leap like Antelope? Women who butcher Wetas with their fingers?

This is what Charbonneau says? This is his trickery? Puh, I say. I wish to stay at Metaharta and work.

He does not *say*, she says, he signs to me. Otter Woman begins to show me how he signs then stops. He is no good at it.

She tries again.

He signs, Corn Women will eat you. She points at me with her chin. And then Charbonneau does this. She picks up a Corn cob and holds it to her teeth. She clumsy-fuddles. He signs, Corn Women will eat you with their, and then he says, *Nubbley* Corn teeth.

Otter Woman goes back to her sewing.

Why does he sign when he speaks Hidatsa? He said, Nubbley Corn teeth?

Yes, he says those words. He does not speak Hidatsa good.

She stops sewing and begins to laugh. Corn Women will eat you with their nubbley Corn teeth, she sputters. He is crazy.

She laughs. We laugh. We laugh and laugh. We laugh crying.

When we are finished, and I am alone, I remember the Hidden Sisters of Mandan. No one goes there. They are *Spirit Beings* who live in the Sky. He cannot take me there.

Charbonneau weights me with Buffalo hides while he carries nothing but his musket. Each day, he eyes my body and snuckles his drool. He waits for my breasts to puff, for my Woman time to come. I hunch my shoulders and crater my chest.

We have been here sixteen Moons, Otter Woman tells me. You are his spring carrot.

I will work in Mandan Corn fields while Charbonneau trades and barters.

Mandan Corn is as beautiful as trade beads, Corn the color of Sky and clay and summer grasses. Mandan Corn Women are more beautiful than Bawitchuwa. They shimmer like raw Corn. But they do not speak to me unless they insult me. The People of the First Man have no breath for Snakes.

I talk to myself as I work. Your fields are pitiful, I say. Puh. This Corn, these Beans are nothing. I work down long rows that swallow me. If Running Woman were here, I say louder, you would not be mean. She is bigger than all of you. Stronger.

Sleeping Deer rise and bound from me—rustle-clather, rustle-clather, rustle-clather. Other sounds shake me. Snorts and growls that sound like Weta but are not Weta. Squeak voices. Earth rumbles. I turn and see only leaves swacking. What-was-there now gone.

When Corn rows grow dark and darker, Charbonneau whistles for me, and Corn Women smile as wide as River bends. Next time we send you to our Hidden Sisters. Our Sisters will slice you in two with their razor Corn leaves. You will not brag there. They will cut your tongue out.

I whimper beside Man-who-plagues-us. Le poupon, he says.

When Debai lips to Earth, Otter Woman seeks Alive Beside Arrow. They walk and plan their ways. They laugh and tease. They are One, Otter Woman tells me. I do not ask how.

I tell Otter Woman I will find Too Ott Lok before I leave. She does not listen.

Charbonneau does not care if Otter Woman remakes herself with another. She tends to him, makes his food, takes off his leggings and his moccasins when he returns. Otter Woman rolls with Charbonneau when he wants. He leaves me be.

Days of change

Lost His Head to Horse threads grasses, a razor snake, his belly smeared with mud. He comes so close I hear cracks of his smile. His teeth flash like small strikes of Lightning.

You are close to your blood time, Otter Woman tells me. That is why he bothers you. I told you. I told you, you should not talk to him. He will plague you more than Charbonneau. Your blood scent calls. Men keen to Women change are like Fish in clear Water startled by shadows. They smell All Around.

You are mine, Lost His Head to Horse hisses. He no longer makes me laugh. Saliva salvers his tongue. He pulls out his penis and shakes it at me. He is bitter silvery slobber.

I do not give him power.

Otter Woman is no help. Her pleasure with Alive Beside Arrow is as loud as rattle gourds. She wraps her legs around Alive Beside Arrow and he yells out of fear, and bliss-ruckus, that she will gouge him or break the arrow. They pant together. They soil each other. They make noise again and again. I am sick with their rumbles.

Lost His Head to Horse fears Otter Woman. When she bumps him, he wobbles and shakes, and guards his soft skull.

Go away, I tell him. Do not plague me.

Otter Woman shutters and tithes all of herself to Alive Beside Arrow.

She is so loud in her sex pleasure Lost His Head to Horse skitters away holding his head.

One Eye moves in and out of Trees, twisty as a sapling, squatting long to listen to White Men talk trade. Otter Woman and Alive Beside Arrow do not see One Eye or hear grasses swish. I fear he will kill Otter Woman for her bold ways.

|He is woman| tells me trouble comes up River.

I crouch in grasses with River Otters and Lightning snakes to watch White Men. I am like One Eye who watches. I watch. I listen. White Men smoke and gadder and laugh too hard and piss near me. I fear they will rootle me out. My belly quakes like shallow Water Ogres sniff.

Pink-faced Men from Northwest Trading Company and Hudson Bay call themselves French and British and Spanish and Americans. Some dress like Indians but are blind to the People's ways. They snort their arrival. White Men call us redskins, good-for-nothing Indians and call themselves Indians to other White Men. They know good and bad Beaver pelts but they do not know Tribal People from Indians. They speak about their perilous journeys over precipitous cliffs. They tell of the dangers they face in Indian Country.

To our faces they speak our names. They fail.

Hidden in piss grass I learn their slaughter-words for Women.

Cunt .. Muff .. Kitty .. Mink Trap .. Gash .. Fanny .. Beaver ..

Pussy .. Axe Wound .. Penis Trap .. Tuppence .. Fuck .. Mount ..

Cock Scratch .. Diddle Hole .. Twat .. Ebonpoint Saddle .. Boobies .. Jubblies .. Globes .. Jugs .. Dilly Plugs .. Wound .. Fish .. Fish Cave .. Fish Straw .. Squaw ..

I am only safe beside Charbonneau.

I am not safe at all.

Corn Necklace stands outside her Lodge and trembles in the dust-rise of white men passing. Women, easy marks for Wolves, step from their Lodges as white men look to trade, and traders look to trade them.

Women sit on the butcher edge, the slicing cut, the tumble, the lurch, our perilous plummet over the precipitous cliff. There is danger All Around. Everywhere white men. Everywhere trade men. Everywhere Indians wanting what white men have. Only white men do not trade themselves.

You should not be where eyes watch you and Alive Beside Arrow, I tell Otter Woman. It is not our way.

Should I be like you and hide in bush to spy on white man? she answers. What do you know, my Sister?

We are Agaidika. It is *our way* to survive. I will make us survive. I will eat Fish hooks to save us.

Blue Elk will come for us and bring us home, I tell her. We must wait.

Oh, Sister, she says with big eyes, you dream of eating Agai when Buffalo is plenty.

Day of no-good Enemy lies

Old Woman teeters toward camp. She scowls like a trapped Wolverine. I work on weaving my basket tight enough to hold Water. She keeps her tremble eyes on me. I look up at Debai and then I look back to my basket. I do not see her again until I see her moccasined feet in front of me.

She clunks my head with her knife handle.

I hear you ask about Running Woman, she says. I have walked all day from Mandan Camp to visit you. I know Running Woman. When she talks about your pitiful People she spits.

Old Woman strikes me again. You are the same bad.

I gave her my best robes, my fattest Buffalo humps. I let her warm her hands between my legs when she was cold. How does she repay me? She runs off with a skunk trader. She was so ugly no one else would have her.

I do not wish trouble. I slip my awl in the top of my basket and twist.

S—s-nake, she calls me. Good for only slave.

I do not look at her. She wants to jangle me.

She squats beside me and pushes her face close to me. Her rot tooth winks in her mouth like a whistle bone. Her blind eye twitches. Her other eye puckers. I smell gunpowder, edges of buckled Corn. Tiny flies flit around her raggedy shawl.

I do not know how she found me or what she wants.

She whispers to me with her Badger-claw voice. I lie. I lie to you and you are too stupid to know. Too too stupid Shoshoni girl. Do you want to know what happened to Running Woman?

I do not look up. I keep to my basket weaving.

She was sly, that one. She ran away three times. The third time she stole my knife. This knife, she tells me. Old Woman strikes me on the head again with the knife handle. Clunk Clunk Clunk.

She thought she was so good looking she could get away with taking.

Chief's son should have killed the bitch the first time. Four Men tracked her. Four fool Men. They almost overlooked her hiding spot. Shame. If she had not stolen my knife and another's Horse, she would have been forgiven.

Old Woman presses her thumb to her nose and blows snot on the ground beside me. She goes on talking.

You know how they found her? she asks, not wanting my answer. They found her by the root marks she left, but they were piss-poor trackers.

When she reached the Mountains she thought she was safe. What a mistake! She should have gone on.

She killed a Buffalo with stolen bow and arrows. She built a solid hut from green branches. She prepared a stock of dried food. She would have lasted the long winter. These four Men could not have done what she did. They were not worthy to lance her breast. Not worthy to bring her head back to camp on a pole.

Do you know what I did with her head? Do you?

Heat steamed up my robe like quuteyai-mea.

I pulled her ugly head down from the pole by its hair.

She was not so pretty then. She was not so strong. She was nothing but thief. I kicked out her eyes so she will not see light. I kicked the no-good thief into darkness where she belongs. I tossed her mealy head to boys to kick.

I boulder Old Woman's legs to fall her. I grip her squirm tongue and pull. I will tear her tongue from her lies.

Women surround me. Corn Necklace wails.

Old Woman wrestles to keep her tongue.

I reach down her throat with the storm of my spite. I feel her gritted kidney, the tremble-piss of curdled liver.

Women push at me. Try to rustle between. I hold on. Her shoulders are wide and hard-brittle. Old Woman's heart thumps like drum strikes in Canyons. She is one who has battled many. She scratches and bites and claws me. I hold on.

I feel the breath-wet puff of Bia's voice in my ear. *My Baide. You have won.*

I let go.

White Clay Women help Old Woman stand. She wobbles and pushes them away and then she spits at my feet.

I twitch like a Rabbit, like a Mountain Cat in a snare, like a Woman who wants War.

All night, Coyote plays bone games outside Charbonneau's Lodge and speaks in the voices of my Relations. *Trouble comes. Trouble comes. Trouble comes. Trouble comes.*

Day of running

Traders talk of going home. They travel from far far away. They say their seas are bigger than our Prairies. They have seen Fish bigger than Buffalo. If they have boated and walked more miles than I have traveled with Enemy, I will go home too.

I will steal knives and bows and best Horse. I will not stop or leave root sign. I will find Too Ott Lok and take him to Combs Gut. I will tell stories of Running Woman, of Her last great run I will finish.

Corn Necklace waits for me by Lodge door at Debai rise.

She places a necklace made of Blue Corn woven with red fabric around my neck.

Her voice is low. Quick. You will find Too Ott Lok at the center of Mandan. He lives with the revered People.

I do not believe her.

You are brave to attack Folds Over, she tells me. She is like Raccoon who enters Villages unafraid, all fire and snarl tooth. She is also one who seeks revenge. She is not to be troubled with. Gunpowder slivers her eyes. She is blinded by poor want. What will become of our Children if Women kill over a Squash knife or musket ball? My Aunties say at one time Women did not fight over small no-matters. Before Small Pox fell us, sneaking beneath our Lodges, covering our People in sores, we believed we could *see* our Enemies.

Now it is always dim night. We mistake each other for Enemy. Now Women watch.

If you leave, she tells me. You must watch for Enemies All Around.

Day I chose to survive

I fool Charbonneau and trick Otter Woman. I pretend I am busy working, busy tending to Squash and Pumpkins, digging roots, gathering seeds. I visit Corn Necklace and we laugh together. But I watch River Men comings and goings. I keep my eye on Women setting up for trade. I brush their Horses and help them pack goods.

I sew moccasins for my journey home and hide them beneath Corn sheaths. I watch Horses closely. One sleepy-eye Horse is tied with only fray rope. He will do. No one will see him gone. He eats tall grasses and pitters off far. No one will look to find him gone. Children climb his back and he does not shiver.

In my tall willow basket I hide jerky under nest-grass. I snatch untended food—meat scraps for dogs, squash and berries left to dry. White gristle chew from babies.

I know every Water seam, every twirling current. I work. I smile. I sing. Corn silk powders my hair, my face, and I become no one to be watched. I make like I am tame. I make like I am broken.

I watch for Lost His Head to Horse. He fiddles in capture mud. He clatters after me. I hear his foot stomp long before I spy him. I can outrun this diddle.

One Eye lizards me too. Through bush thatch and shivering Trees, he follows. When I step from sweat Womb and steam, and jump in River, I see him squinting in the tall reeds. Watching.

I watch back.

I work close to Charbonneau's Lodge today.

As we cut Squash and Pumpkin I ask Corn Necklace about One Eye who watches. I no longer trust what Lost His Head to Horse tells me. He wishes to hobble me with scare stories.

Corn Necklace keeps to task. She does not answer.

When Moon becomes a sliver and trade men barter, we busy ourselves where no one keeps their eyes on us.

Corn Necklace whispers, He is Chief of White Clay. Chief of People of the Willows. Both his wives left him. He chased one to Mandan, it is said, and split her skull with an axe.

Lost His Head to Horse did not lie.

Did he kill the other wife? I ask.

She looks at me with the wide stone eyes of a Corn doll. No. He gave her many Horses.

What is his name? I ask.

He is Le Borgne, she says, but he has many names. White Men call him Cyclops. Why do you ask?

He follows me, I tell her. I do not think she believes me.

Day of new seeds and new Birds

|He is woman| runs to me like Antelope with fluttering wings. Look at me, *She* says, I am alight with streamers fashioned from bits of fabric from traders. Look at what they've given me. *She* twirls and dances around me. I am full of surprises, *She* says. You should get used to surprises, Little Storm. You have many coming.

I try to follow what *She* is saying but *She* flitters like a grasshopper. *She* ducks like a gopher. *Her* words are murky. All Around *Her* is puckery light like Water after ice melts.

I bring words: glitter, glisten, sparkle, twinkle, shimmer, shine, tumultuous, victory, stupendous. My favorite word . . de-li-cious, *She* says. The next time I see you, you will remember.

So what words have you brought me? *She* asks.

Do you know where Too Ott Lok is? I ask.

I do not know a Too Ott Lok, *She* says. Is that a word?

She scatters around Village like Milk seeds. Skitters past baskets of tidbits. Ruffles great stacks of Beaver pelts and Buffalo hides. The People gaze at *Her* in wonder and awe. One scruff trader tries to catch *Her* and *She* pushes his head down and leaps over him.

Tinkle. Tinkle. *She* lifts a bell from *Her* necklace and shakes it. Tinkle, tinkle, tinkle, *She* says and runs off.

But I have seen |He is woman| walk among the People in deepest quiet. *She* brings *Herself* to the People like healing, like Womb sleep. Like Trickster.

|He is now Many| does not parade *Himself*. *He* is so powerful, *His* power shimmers off *Him* like smoke. When *He* passes, the People touch *Him*. But there are days when *He* threads through the Villages without sound or breeze. Women stop still when *He*

chickers between their Lodges like the scent of willows and lily Water, the faint whiff of Skunk. I tell no one *He* is my teacher.

|He is man| speaks for the People. *He* moves among us like Mountain Lion and mouse. No one is his Enemy.

Days of hiss talk and no Buffalo

Men return storm-eyed with pitiful Deer and runt Elk. It is the
Season to Gather. To store up.

No one has seen Buffalo or Wolves who attend Buffalo.

There is fear talk. Buffalo talk. In Lodges All Around the
People gather. Commotion all day. All night. Songs of Buffalo.

Buffalo do not rumble Villages. Buffalo stay their distance.

In Ceremony, Buffalo will return, they sing.

I see *Weta* running beside River, clawing Cottonwood Trees.
She leaves her hair on bark.

In Mandan and Metaharta, beautiful Women have become
ripe in their Womanness. Their voices are whispery as Water
shallows—berry-sweet, root-crisp. They gather behind Trees
where River backs into pools and big Fish chumble beneath
green branches. They run naked in and out of Water. They
scurry-butt here, there. They back up to each other and Coyote
laugh. *Snickhiss. Snickhiss. Snickhiss.* They show each other
what. They laugh so hard they fall into one another.

They should not make fun of Ceremony, Old Women say. They
will chase away Buffalo.

Young Women say they do not wish to fuck Old Men to pass
power to Husbands. If he can call Buffalo from our cunts—Power
is ours.

Pakit pakit pakit, the Old Women scold. No good will come
of jokes.

Beneath green cool, Women flurry together as small bits,
Cottonwood seed spirals, gathered
winnowers. Women gather beauty All Around.

We collect power for our Children, they whisper.

Corn Necklace has been tatter-mouthed for days. She returned from Ceremony with Badger scowl. Beautiful Women flutter her. Tease her. She does not laugh.

Something is wrong, I tell myself. These Women bad-joke the Sacred. I would not cuss my People's Ceremony.
Lost His Head to Horse stands in shadows close to me.
I must leave. Soon.

Days to know and remember

To know People, Appe told me, you must watch them. You must see them in all their ways. You must see them in their weakness.

To know yourself, Bia told me, you must watch People. You will know what awaits you if you attend to others. You will know your want.

I watch Men at Mandan braid Horse tail hair into their own hair until their hair becomes as long as travois behind them. They gloat on their beautiful Horses with their hair so long it rivers. One Man's hair rips off beneath the stomp of another Man's Horse. He does not pity his torn scalp. He lifts his head higher.

Women joke. Unlaughing. If Men had babies their hair would be snarl-knots, they say.

The Men are beautiful to me. Their hair glistens like Water falls. I stop my work to watch them pass.

You gawk because you are young, the Women tell me. When you are older you will see their foolishness. I see Blue Elk coming toward me, his hair sweeping the ground.

Corn Necklace's Husband, Broke Leg, kneads his wife, Many Teeth, while two babies suck her enormous teats. I hear squeals from her Lodge.

She likes sex, Corn Necklace, says. She sings and squeals as he huffs over her.

Many Teeth is the favored wife.

Inside Charbonneau's Lodge .. I smell Otter Woman's detest, her Womb-sick
longing for Alive Beside Arrow.

Heat spills the milk scent of Charbonneau and Otter Woman to his Horses. His wick sprinkle. The Fish and birth curds of their together.

Horses snuffle. Jostle. Stamp.

Inside me is an empty nest where flapping Birds swoop-steal sticks.

On full Moon nights, I hear together-laughter of Men and Women. Grunt of their sharp breaths. Their lap swats. Their rut storm.

I dream Blue Elk returns from the Hunt. His skin is burning grass, dry suckle berries, roots breaking dry Earth with open mouths. I smell him. His sluice rises between my legs.

My Womb draws like a cut.

Days of Mandan Corn Women

Corn Necklace sneaks up beside me. She has walked from Metaharta to Mandan. I have been working long days among Corn Women while Charbonneau gadders and makes trade deals.

Do not say a word, Corn Necklace signs, and nods for me to follow. She hides in the Corn with dog eyes, and waits. She waits and waits.

Mandan gardens are bigger than Metaharta gardens. Here Fox and Coyotes hunker down in the long rows and birth. Birds swoop down over the rows and wobble away carrying Corn cobs the size of my arm. I dig pit seeds from gourds and Pumpkins and Squash. Clean seeds from pulp string. My fingers pucker. My fingernails loosen. I scrape and pull. My knife blade dulls under mountains of Pumpkins. All day shredding and pulling tough Corn leaves.

I work alone but guarded. Corn Women snigger when they near.

I work beside a big Woman named Corn Grease who can out-run me. The Women here harvest baskets and baskets of Corn. They trade their Corn to other tribes. They feed their Husbands and their families.

Charbonneau has paid Corn Grease a handful of beads to watch me while he trades to make sure I stay where he says I stay. Corn Grease squats beside me, cracks Pumpkins like eggs. She scoops out guts with hands as big as Cougar paws. She finishes four before I open one. She lines up gut string like combed hair. When she is done, she drops Pumpkin plop into great copper boil pots.

Run, Corn Grease says. White man means nothing to me. When I run she runs behind so fast she clips my heels. She laughs when I tumble. Her funny is mean.

I am pitiful. My hair a matt of gut pulp. I am sweat-stink sour. It is no good to sit in Corn fields with Women who mock. I have not grown used to their cruelty.

Corn Necklace lifts her hand. Come, she whispers.

Corn Necklace scoops Water over my head at River and then brushes my hair with hands like Bia. I have been cruel to her. I shake tiny shakes. My chest quakes. She Smudges me. She pats my hand.

We prepare you, she says. She offers prayers to all Four Directions.

Corn Necklace leads me through thatches of saplings. We go on past heroic walls of carved snakes. Turtle stone peckings. Stories carved in rock cliffs. We go on. Up beyond River. Past scour brush and root carrots. On up where Earth dries and opens. My moccasins are powdered with dust.

We pass Ceremonial Lodges of girls, Sacred Burning grasses, Women-awaken Songs, prayers. Corn Necklace stands beside me when she sees me gawp at Bias blessing the solemn changes of their Daughters.

We walk through sparrow-lit Trees until we come to the camp of hump-backed Women, their faces knuckle-pocked.

Corn Necklace does not lower her voice. White men never see Women in the Lodges at the edges of Numakiki Villages, she says. They are Women who carried the Small Pox Dead to scaffolds and lost their fingers to cleansing fires. Women who gathered great bundles of sticks in the frost-bitten winters of fever. Their fires reached the Sky. They are only Witches to white men, only Women who crawl hump-backed, only pull dogs who carry meat, their hands only palms, the webbed feet of ducks.

Now they tend to the fires of *the Lost* who died from Pox.

The Many Spirit People tend to them and the Mandan Corn Women.

Pass through here quickly, she whispers.

We climb and climb and Corn Necklace reaches for my hand to pull me. We reach top of giant bluff where we see All Around. She leads me on and farther. On past knuckle grass and Milk stem, on past needle grass and raider's wort until we come to place Beyond All Things. We overlook a Valley of Corn so vast, so wide, Hawks sail overhead.

As Debai lifts Sky, Songs lift from Corn fields. Their voices sweet as berries. Sweet as spearmint on hot days. The Hidden Corn fields not be seen by Enemy, not be seen by white men. I tremble here. Who am I to come here?

Walk softly, Corn Necklace says.

We thread hillside down to Prairie below.

Corn is so high it pierces Sky.

Angry Crows call overhead.

The old stories move in me like light flickers into night.

. . ..

Coyote stands in a field when Crows descend. He sees one here, then there—small specks of dust in the Sky. He thinks they are a dust storm but when He looks closer, He sees flapping wings. All Around. All Around. All Around. All Around Him. They lift Coyote with their great flapping wings. They surround Him. He is inside of Himself. He is outside of Himself. He is changed from Life to Death, from Death to Life.

ă'-rah

Crows are furious they cannot snipe Corn. They cannot get close.

Beautiful Women, taller than Men, sing Songs from their high-poled watches. Their Song spills over Bean blossoms, shivers over Squash and rolls on, on into distant fields. Corn Woman's Song is so dizzying tassels of Corn ripple. Huge cut Pumpkins dry beneath Debai, their fragrance so sweet Crows wobble. Sunflower heads are so large and heavy, they droop to be picked. I have never seen so much plenty. I shield my eyes to look up at the Women on their high scaffolds.

Do not stare, Corn Necklace says. You will become blind.

Mandan Corn Women voices crack down down down down over fields. Their voices rumble in my chest. All Birds fluster away. Not Crow.

Corn Necklace leads me down Corn rows. Leaves flutter over us. No one could find us here. Every row leads to many shade paths that go on and on.

A Woman wanders through Corn, unafraid of lost. A long yellow strip stains the front of her woven robe. The fringes of her robe are Corn silk. Her breastplate is made of Blue Corn.

Corn Necklace nods to the Woman.

The People say she flies over Mandan Corn fields, Corn Necklace says.

Corn Necklace holds back a curtain of leaves. Do not be afraid, she says. No white man can enter here.

Is this a trick? I boulder myself.

In gopher-darkness of Lodge-high Corn, Debai flashes between stalks. Bells tinkle. Someone thatches in and out of light, in and out of green blackness, and comes closer ..

The Man is as tall as a sapling and as slender as a Corn stalk. I have not seen him before and yet, He weaves toward me. Is it |He is now Many|?

When He comes into light, He is as beautiful as Blue Elk—His eyes polished with Corn-tassel light. His lips stained and plump. He is dressed in white buckskin. Colorful streamers flow from His shoulders. Small bells jingle at His ankles.

It cannot be.

I see Him. I see Him for who He is.

Too Ott Lok?

I step closer.

I touch His beautiful hair woven with beads and painted strands.

He stands without talk and lets me look. My eyes water and then spill.

Yes. He says low. Yes. It is I.

Too Ott Lok. Too Ott Lok, my Brother.

I lose strength.

He holds my hands and I cry and cry.

I was not good to you, I say. I was mean. I left you.

Do not cry, He says. I am here to help others. I am here to live with Many Spirit.

When I travel with Charbonneau, we pass the great Lodge of the Many Spirit People. Their Lodge is twined with Sweetgrass and Sage. A good smell is All Around. My bones become as light as dry grass. I could flitter away like Cottonwood fluff.

Too Ott Lok lives with |He is now Many| and the others in the Lodge who bring quiet.

Too Ott Lok's face is wise and kind now, not plagued by Moppo. Where are the pests who plague you? I ask. Where is fat-cheeked Too Ott Lok?

He laughs. It is fat Too Ott Lok grown. It is baby-cry Too Ott Lok who plagued you.

He smiles. I have a say now. I tell you, in the Not-far, I will send you a gift.

What gift? I ask.

You will know, He says. You will know the gift is from me. Remember.

I cannot tell you what will be, Too Ott Lok tells me. I do know you will go on, my Sister. Your journey will be long and you will be free. You will see me now. I am healed.

Corn Woman Song wings down Bird-like, soft as feathers, soft as Corn silk. *Weta* rustles Corn. I hear but do not see her.

Wind whirls.

Too Ott Lok turns from me, shifts, and is gone.

Day of good work

No one looks beyond low Corn fields to higher ground.

The high Mandan fields are safe from Crows and prying eyes, safe from snatching predators, safe from white men.

I know now. All things balance. Cruelty is not the good way.

I am not alone in my pile of Corn husks. I am not alone in lower Mandan fields. Thousands of mice scritter and scratch beneath me, All Around. I thank them as I gather mouse beans hidden in sleeping sheaths of Corn leaves.

Corn Women laugh like I am one of many fools.

What good are you to Earth? Corn Daughter says. You only gather what belongs to Earth. You steal from mice. They tease me. They gather seeds and berries too. Their baskets are heavy with roots.

Corn Daughter lifts her robe and a Corn cock juts at me. She lifts her robe higher and her nipples dribble Corn kernels like slow rain.

She laughs.

I laugh.

I am scarecrow. I am no power to their mighty show. I have no children. I am no power to all they seed.

Children gather around Corn Grease, and she opens her mouth to show them Corn cobs rise from her throat.

When Corn Women are among Men, Men bow their heads to them like an Elk-buck who has lost battle.

Day I am no more my own

You smell like Wolf tongue, Otter Woman tells me.
She sniffs my breath.
Are you bleeding? Does your belly ache?
I shake my head.
Girls taken become Women before they are Women. Clean yourself. Make sure Old Gruff does not snuffle your wind.
But it is my suffer time. Charbonneau lights on me, scatters my Womb blood.
Otter Woman pushes him from me but he wins. He strikes her down and boulders me. Her cheek bleeds. I do not wish my Sister harm. I grab her hand and tell her no.
Otter Woman cries.
Charbonneau huffs over me like a stack of burning bones. My blood sizzles. If all the kettle fires died and frozen wood could not kindle a lick of flame, I would not be cold. My blood would sear the Lodges of my Enemy. The killing heat of my breath would strike fire no Enemy could douse.
When Charbonneau sleeps, I do not look for Horse. I do not search out long-collect cache.
In dark night, I run beneath Star glitters. I run along River. I hear stumble-puff of running near me. Rustle. Crack. Rustle. Crack.
Weta.
I will run barefoot into Mountains. I will run to Blue Elk. *Weta* runs with me.
My heart roars in my chest. I gulp air and run, run. I stumble and run. I slap aside swatting brush. I jump rocks. Stone Ogres gawk at me from their stone houses, and I run on. I run into the dark Woods. I run without fear of *Wood* or *Water Spirits*.
A Star jabs black night and runs across Sky to follow me.
I run until I can no longer run.

I gather twigs and grasses for my bed. No fire. Charbonneau would find me. Lost His Head to Horse would find me. My body chatters. Moon light chickers on River swirls. I close my eyes. I pray. I ask *she-who-cannot-be-named* to guard me.

I smell *Weta* near me, around me, and sleep comes. Sleep.

Sacred Earth dreams in me

I am both awake and asleep and a voice neither my own nor Bia's nor Appe's nor Flatbird's speaks to me from Water, from fire, from all Four Directions. The voice is the sound of wind when wind stirs low grasses and then moves, and moves, faster and stronger and stronger and causes Earth to rise to dust.

Daughter,
know
there are times when the ground rolls
                                        and the great houses shake.
Tassels of Corn rain pollen. For on the shelf of Earth___
Buffalo riot.
Skulls of their hooves
                dent   mark   cut
                    the Land.
Buffalo are a wide river and the dust-shaken Earth
becomes smoke
a hundred Prairie fires
                        dust
                        rolling
                        up
                        so
                        high
                    wind splays
                    limbs of trees
                    pines hiss
                    crack.
Even the bones of the Earth cannot stand the weight of Buffalo running.

The whole Village gathers
in the Earth-quaking roar of Buffalo   passing.
In the murky wall of Buffalo dusk   great clouds bloom.
Buffalo charge the Sky
Snorting breath
trailing shreds grass scents
A rumbling storm of hooves. How can they churn Lightning
rush the Sky?
Hoof flint. Fire stone
a field of fire
beneath them.
There is a sound Buffalo make as They scrape
night ground
stirring
wind.
The sound is
War whoops
Women crying
deep gut
rising.
Pain carves
a deeper throat than Canyons
a tunnel
of a thousand trampled
Weasels
Rabbits
Deer
that ride the current of Buffalo wind.
Even Antelope cannot flee Buffalo running.
So many Buffalo running Sky twists
sheer silver

channels
of wind.

Heavy hooves sharpen stones
spark
fire.

A hard night run with the glow of hooves striking Earth until
Earth becomes a glaze of heat.
See the horizon lit with flames of Buffalo.
Buffalo create storm Lightning
and
low
to the Earth
Buffalo create heat that carves the Earth.
As the Edge of the great herd widens they become an arrow of
Buffalo shooting across Prairies.

Smell .. singed hair stinging Earth ..
See, my Daughter, the press and move of Buffalo, their grunt and push.
Buffalo seared with pitch coat becoming Lightning static snap of
their own wooly bodies.
Or they become like kerosene
a searing line
wild
Buffalo become hot rainbow fire.

The crazy crazy wondrous wind of them rising   calves lifting   in
the dizzy tornado
of a thousand Buffalo
The Sky pushed back.

Only the old stories
wet in the breath of the dying
speak the day Buffalo crowned the Village.
A great circle story goes round
the wheel of charging Buffalo.

Buffalo appear everywhere.
above
below.
A herd snarling with lights, cracking, shuddering All Around.

Even Hills surrender to Buffalo.

    Our children broke   like wind-splintered trees
    Sheer weight of sound   our Lodges exploded
        surrounding us
Our Warriors could not save the People
        Buffalo advanced.

    The People became   blue smoke   a hazy morning so soon gone.
        A whole People vanished.

    Only their *Spirits* stay   in the kicked-Earth fog.
no tears
no crying
no fearful shouts
or shriek of Women cradling Daughters.

Earth wounded by great Buffalo sweeping through the great
Lodge camp.
Spirits whisper there
still

there
there
the restless place
the white men travel
through.

When Buffalo dust clears, a small girl wobbles alone on the vast trampled Earth. She trembles. Buffalo calves nudge her.

She holds on to the beard of a Buffalo bull to keep herself standing.

I snort awake.

Now All Around

Yellow leaves rain down over me, around me. Flower-scented Water glints around the roots of Turtle grass and Cattails. I try to shake off shudder sparks of dreaming but I cannot tell if I am awake or asleep. If I am sleeping, I have slept into the light of day.

When you dream in now-around-you, be watchful, Appe said. You are close to our long-ago Relations.

I gather myself to a sound so faint, so effervescent, the sound the squeer-squeak Sky makes when it melts with light. |He is woman| told me white men call this Sky the Northern Lights. The People know it is the voice of *the Sky People*.

A hundred small mirrors wink and flash.

I shelter my eyes and see a child squinting, holding her hands above her eyes.

Is it me? Could it be? I have not seen myself in white man's mirror.

Ah, a voice says, now you see yourself as others see you.

Who is near? I ask.

Rustle. Rustle. Rustle. Through smoke-glimmer-haze, I see an Old Woman cover herself with a blanket made of leaves. Beside her, campfire flames lick Sky.

Old Woman's eyes are liver sheen. She is blind. Mirrors flash on her moccasins, on her head kerchief, on her dress made of sagebrush bark. Small winds eddy around her with a scent like Sunrise Water, long little click of blue fly, root prayer, heart blood.

What are you running from? she asks.

I am quiet.

She drops her blanket. Faces move over her mirror dress. I see Otter Woman crying. Alive Beside Arrow beside her. Debai breaks over fields where they walk.

Look closely, she says. Her voice chimes branches in high forests, blows ice-grass whistles.

I see Water. Waves and waves of Water.

Remember, she tells me. Remember what you see. You will long to see it again.

I do not wish to see Water. I wish to see Blue Elk.

Old Woman cups both hands beneath her breasts.

Mirrors blind, chicker, and I see blue-black shining hair. Blue Elk. I see Blue Elk.

Can he see me?

She laughs. No, she says.

Has she come to take me back to Man-who-plagues-us?

Charbonneau? No. I like Old Grunt better. Oof is awful. But true.

Old Woman lifts her blind eyes to weak Debai. It will rain. Good, she says.

She wobbles to standing.

When we enter deep-dark woods, she does not walk in darkness. Her mirrors catch light, Water glare, Tree shine, stone polish, puddle glint, grass sparkle.

Trees sigh as we pass. It is so dark in the woods, red spots dance before me. I walk in a fawn mewl of blindness.

Your Appe was right, she says. Weta is All Around.

I do not ask how she knows. When Old Woman speaks, mirrors catch days long gone. Appe, Bia. In one mirror White Crow walks with Old Woman. Her face flitters from mirror to mirror. Alive. Unbroken White Crow.

Old Woman goes on walking. Long ago is not long ago, she says. Her voice breaks like Bird Song. Long ago is with us now, as are the days that lead on.

Men don't need to become intoxicated with white man's power or war. Come close to young Women and you will smell white clay, the strong and odorous white-spike marsh flower, green sugar root, sweet stinging nettle, poison dizzy vine.

Women glisten like rain in spider webs, like the thousand-colored grasshoppers in spring fields. Men are blinded by our power. Open your eyes I say to Men. Open wide.

But Women, ah, Women go on seeing. We see even when we are blind.

We climb and climb but Old Woman does not slow or wind. As she walks she makes a sound like creek Water, like stittering bees, like stones tumbling together beneath Water.

She is quiet a long time and when she looks at me again she is sighted. Her eyes are as clean as a baby's. Round with wonder of all that will be. Kind. Uncorrupted.

My Daughter, Old Woman says, when you go on the white man's long journey, they will see their safety as your only worth. They will catalog and collect. They will name the Sacred places.

Long ago, the People knew Life rested in what *must-not-be-named*. When all things are named, when all Earth's gifts are claimed without thanks, without stories, without prayer, Water and fire will come. Pray to all Four Directions. Pray to heal the desecrated path.

Across her mirrored gown I see a skitch of light out of darkness, a strange skittering.

A Monster made of Lightning walks up River toward Mandan
.. Boom.

Each Lightning strike is He. Boom ..

Each Thunder smack His step. Boom ..

He lights the pale bluffs like Debai. Boom ..

He is coming.

Rain falls All Around. Rain quivers down. Dust smoke rises. Old Woman turns and turns and her glittering mirrors become the glittering River, the glittering wet grasses, the glittering Tree sap, the glittering waves of the faraway glittering sea.

MANDAN FORT

Day of white man come like War

Up up up the River, they come. Guns flare with fire, they come
.. Boom.

Soft Earth shudders .. Boom.

Dirt beads swirl down to River and smoke back up to us ..
Boom.

They are spectacle. A strut display. White men stand up in their
boats and their gun smoke streams behind them. They are proud as
Mandan Chief Sheheke with new tiddle-bits. Proud as Men who
tie Horse hair into their braids. They are not like the taggle traders
who skulk Villages and hawk Buffalo robes and tinkle jewels. These
white men come like War.

Beautiful Warriors on Horses line the bluff. Children peek
through legs. Cower. Men and Women slide down to River on a
plume of white clay dust.

Charbonneau sputters, enfin d'autres hommes dignes. He pre-
tends he does not care, but he is the first fool to scramble to the
overlook and gawk.

I hide in tall grasses with Otter Woman to watch goings-on.

Too Ott Lok finds us and we tell him to get down.

They are different from other white men, Too Ott Lok says.
What do they come for?

They come like dance, Otter Woman, says. They want us to
see them.

|He is woman| runs toward us, *Her* robe glimmering with
shells and oiled quills, *Her* shoulders trailing ribbons. *She* waves to
Too Ott Lok and joins us in soft grasses.

We cannot hide with |He is woman|. *She* glitters like River at first light. *She* strikes rocks together and lights *Her* kinnikinic pipe. I cover my head with my shawl.

Look, look, red coats with shiny buttons, *She* says. Why do they wear regalia? Oh, these men! They do not wish to trade; they wish to show off.

They shamed one of their own, whipped him bloody in front of the Arikara.

We turn to face |He is woman|, who knows everything. |He is woman| crushes dry Rabbit brush between *Her* fingers and presses it to *Her* lips, and *Her* lips turn the color of bark. *She* changes like clouds.

Where do all these white men keep their white Women? *She* goes on. Do they have Women? Have you ever seen one of their Women? They must have killed all their Women with their big guns. |He is woman| talks so fast *She* Magpies. *She* has been too long around white man.

|He is woman| turns to Too Ott Lok. You did not tell me you were going to a Celebration. Look. Everyone is here.

You were not in the Lodge, Too Ott Lok says.

She flubbers *Her* lips at Too Ott Lok and he smiles.

Le Borgne knows all, *She* says.

I sit up to listen.

Le Borgne does not trust these men. They're no good. Did you hear . . oh, what did I hear? |He is woman| rubs *Her* head. Interpreters. They want interpreters. And Charbonneau, that snivel dog, would sell his offspring to go.

|He is woman| turns to me. I have not seen you in a while. You are so small. Where's your big belly? *She* sniffs. I pity you, Little Storm. I would not wish to have a baby by a white man. Not that white man.

My stomach is small-pouched. I tell no one, not even Otter Woman, I carry child.

|He is woman| talks and talks. These pitiful white men, all doomed. I see the tiny arrows in their hair. Only Grizzle Hair will live long.

What are you talking about? Too Ott Lok says.

The fools visited the top of *Spirit Mound* after they were told what would happen.

Now everyone turns toward |He is woman|.

The great *Mound* rises out of the Plains beyond Mandan, a lone cliff, a giant neck without a head. When we travel past the *Mound*, Charbonneau kipples in the grass there, like a child turned round and round. Birds shimmer at the edges of its great precipice.

The Arikara say the *Mound* is protected by the Little People, and warn if you climb the *Mound*, the Little People will shoot you with poison arrows. They will curse you to bad Death.

Days after we pass *Spirit Mound*, Charbonneau butcher kicks in sleep. We hear a ring ring wind leak from his head, and Otter Woman and I go outside, and sleep where dogs curl between Lodges.

Maybe the white men fight other Monsters, |He is woman| says. But no one fights the Little People on *Spirit Mound*.

As we watch the happenings below, I feel change come over |He is woman|. I fold myself and cover my belly. *Her* power can wheedle like wind, in and out of Trees, cause dust wheels to spin.

One of their Men will visit our Lodge, *She* says. He hides his true self from others. He comes with shame. He comes with anger. He comes with sodomy. This white man is not one with his own men. He is not one with his self.

This white man comes up River to claim. He is not interested in Beaver pelts or Women. In his eyes, Everything he sees is already his.

I look down River at their shining gun barrels, their proud, pumped chests. Wind comes up River. Rises. Leaves turn and turn and scatter over River, over us.

Boom.

Their boom-puff Thunder *and* Spirit-Lightning *will kill us,* Onion Wife *shouts.*

After the white men are welcomed on shore, I dodge Charbonneau as I weave among the People.

|He is woman| finds me.

Pay attention, *She* says. Listen to everything these white men say. Do not change their words or you will find only muddled thoughts. You must become Word Gatherer. You are wobbly in your knowledge but you do not have much time.

One day you will know, *She* says.

Day of Weta no more

The white men brag they have shot a Bear. Her blood tracks lead off into the Prairie. Her footprints are as large as split Tree trunks. The white men cannot find her. All day I search for her. Grandmother, return *Weta*. Be merciful to *Weta* who saves me.

Day of white men fire

All Chiefs come to listen to white men talk, all Chiefs but Le Borgne.

Le Borgne watches from his always hideaway and sends his Watchers. If white men are not careful, he will stalk them like Cougar. He will axe them with one axe chop.

Lewis and Clark call their selves Captains.

Their men build an open Lodge for everyone to see they are important. The Captains stand before us, proud, on their new wood floor. Their flags Stream in wind above them.

See our great power, the Captains say, we come in peace from the Great White Father. If you do not treat us well, the Great White Father will punish you.

Some of the People come up and touch their shining buttons. The Captains muddle their faces like fluster-boys. What they say is *urgent*. They spray spittle as they speak. We must understand they come with news from the Great White Father. Their white man flag is their Sacred. Nothing is more important than their mission.

If their Great White Father wants us to understand, then where is he? |He is man| shouts. Why should we listen to subchiefs? If you come with such important news, where are our gifts? Why do you bring an Enemy Arikara to smoke beside you?

Close by the Village, Le Borgne's Watchers light a Prairie fire. Fire sizzles grass and runs. The white man's flag flaps and flaps in the fire wind roar but they pay no attention.

Three People are caught up by racing fire. Fire grass whistles around us. We are redlined by fire. Death-smoke smirches the Village, a black-greenish haze that *ghosts* the Land.

White men celebrate their selves, Smudge with body smoke, burnt-stink kidney, Dead People hair smolder.

A half-breed shows off a small wood box he calls his fiddle. When he lifts his fiddle and pulls his bow a sweet voice sings and the People titter and jolt. Another white man dances on his hands. And just when the white man looks around and measures he has lost our attention, Lewis tells us to wait. Just you all wait, one Captain says. You are in for a treat.

Captain Clark is his own treat, a red-haired succulent man, clean as River Trout. Captain Clark steps behind a curtain of white scarves. The People wait. And wait. Some begin to go back to their Lodges. But just when everyone is ready to give up on the white man, he returns with a Giant.

Let me introduce my Man, York, who works for me, Captain Clark calls out.

A giant Man blacker than a smoked kettle, blacker than obsidian arrow tips, and taller than any Man, stands before us. His muscles move beneath his skin like muscles beneath the skin of a great Weta. He is darker than shadows. The People gasp.

I am a wild animal, Black Man says. He hunches over and bares his teeth. Children scream and run.

The half-breed fiddler fiddles and Black Man begins to dance. His jigging steps roar on the wood floor. The white men clap. Their feet drum. Black Man catches up the People in his dance like a whirlwind pulls up Trees. Women cluster around him sick with want.

The People drum, sing and whoop. Men line up their wives to keep company with Black Man.

Clark must be important, the People say, to have such a Man work for him.

Who cares about the piggly white man? Women say. We want Black Man.

All night all night all night all night .. Death roars.

I wake, and in the dark unsettle, with Charbonneau wheezing out his sour breath, I remember White Man. *The Devil comes up River, he said. Can you see him coming? You will see transformations.*

Night of red Sky dancing

You will travel with me, Charbonneau tells Otter Woman. We will cross Mountains, vast Prairies. You will leave here.

Otter Woman lunges at him, stabs his gut with bone awl.

Man-who-plagues-us laughs until she stings his meal with poison root, feeds him Corn with maggots. He shits blood and sprays himself with the tail of his own piss.

Otter Woman will not leave Alive Beside Arrow.

Charbonneau points to me. You go, he signs.

I am weak with child, tremble when I squat. My Appe's hair still twists in the wind of my Captor's Lodge but I live to return.

Sky dances above me. I shout inside. I will return to Blue Elk.

Charbonneau plays games with the white men. I will go with you, he says. I will go. I will stay. I will go. He thinks he will trick them to give him more money.

The white men scoff. We will find another interpreter.

Charbonneau puffs big. He believes he is winning.

Days of white men building Mandan Fort

All Around white men fall Trees.

Trees hiss. Tree bones snap. Branches cry. Pitch oozes and glitters in their houses made of wood bones. There is no fever like the fever of white men building.

Wood dies like animals. Floorboards moan. Cut Trees shift and split and light spills into sleep. I dream Weta is digging. Her claws scratch scratch scratch scratch beneath the Fort buttress.

How can I birth inside wood ribs like an animal eaten? Away from Lodge circle? Away from the People?

Charbonneau does not care who hears his pant. He gropes me. He slobbers. He presses my hand to his cock.

Wither winds rootle into white man's Lodge, but summer fastens to my belly. I push off my robe. In this shelter, not built by Women, the stink of unwashed men calls mice. I smother in the heat of men bodies. Men breath heat.

Animals skitter. Claw walls. Scratch. Dig.

Moon shifts. Winks down.

White men's eyes glitter in darkness. All night white men fear the People, fear River shrieking, fear the rumble hooves of Buffalo.

Otter Woman and I push open barricade doors to welcome all the People.

Come in, come in, we call. Eat everything here.

The golden-skin half-breed Cruzatte plays his fiddle. The People whoop and dance and eat. The big Chiefs stand shoulder to shoulder in front of the fireplace and steal all the fire heat.

Clark introduces York once, twice, a hundred times. The People elbow and push and sidle up next to Black Man. When York growls and chases the children, Men jitter close to measure what he offers.

Giggle-twitching. Wanting his big self to enter them, wanting his Lightning jolt in their loins.

Music and song and laughter and dance. Food and more dance.

Lewis watches his timepiece.

A white man blasts his gun into the glittery Sky. The People flinch and stop dancing.

Otter Woman looks at me. Gunpowder bitter in the Moon-stutter night.

We are dancing. We are living. Why does he shoot his gun? Otter Woman asks.

Man-who-plagues-us nip-pinches our thighs.

When Lewis's timepiece tells him the People go, he makes them.

Days of white men and brute cold

In hour of first feeding when animals turn the color of dust and blue light glimmers on snow, my blood returns stinging.

I am close to birthing.

The white men boats are frozen rocks. Unmovable. Crushed by River running under ice.

Lewis's men burn their pale bellies on stones. Women stand beside hard River to watch crazy men drop hot rocks on ice. Rocks pop, break. Crumble. Water sloshes lips of boats but no boat moves. Then white men burn ice with wood fire. Fire woofs up and up and blackens Cottonwood trunks. Fire roars and fizzles and boats chumble, and then freeze again.

A child stands so close to fire his hair smokes.

Naked Warriors run frozen River, aloof to cold and white men axing ice. Killer rings frost their blue-headed peckers. Their feet split like firewood. They go on playing.

White men stare, pocket their hands near their crotches.

They're a hearty lot, Clark says to Lewis.

These People bear more cold than I thought possible to endure, Lewis answers.

I commit their words to memory.

Lewis shrugs, clips the purple toes off a boy who wears only shrivel-crack antelope skin. In the days that come, the boy's soles will blacken, then flap.

Days when Women are trade

Broke Leg rubs Corn Necklace in Buffalo tallow. Her thighs gleam. Her nipples turn to cluster-squat flowers. Broke Leg throws his best robe over her nakedness.

Her shoulders shake. She begs. She pleads. No, she says. No.

Broke Leg grabs her neck scruff and bashes her head to his chest.

When she throws her leg over Horse's back, her Womb thatch glistens. She covers herself. She covers her face with her hands. Cold wind scatters her hair.

I run to her. I run to tell her she is good and it is good to go to Ceremony. It is good to Walk with Buffalo.

No, she says. I will not go. She pushes me away.

When I get up. Her Husband shoves me down again.

Broke Leg cannot see his already power.

Men weight their wives with Antelope Buffalo Goat make them walk for miles
for one small favor from Lewis and Clark, a trinket, a handful of beads, a promise of plenty.

They are not the Beautiful Women men fight over.

They struggle. They fall. Sharp snow cuts them.

When they reach Mandan Fort they shake with cold. I sit them close to fire but no fire can warm them. They stare into flames until water trails their cheeks.

No one speaks about the Woman killed by Wolves above camp. Even now Wolves sniff her trail marked by the blood of the hundred pounds of Buffalo she carried.

The razor-snarl of their teeth ripped meat from her carry sack. Wolves bit down through her robe, down to her backbone, down to Death.

She still stands. Hard-frozen. Swoop Birds snipe her eyes.

In fog-brutal days when backs of Buffalo scab with ice and small calves fall to skulk Wolves, Lewis and Clark shoot game.

Birds fall from gun-hazy skies. Fawns mewl in frost grass. Red guts steam snow and hooves of Deer and Antelope click in Trees, slaughter-hung high from Wolves. The woods and plains shine with the silver eyes of dead animals.

White men have not cached summer berries, have not split rye grass to seeds or twisted black moss to chew ropes for winter-hungry days.

Day to keep ways

Corn Necklace leaves gifts—her best Squash knife, her blue-beaded belt.

I do not speak to one who does not live Lifeways. I do not speak to one who will not honor her People's Ceremony to Walk with Buffalo.

Corn Necklace comes for me on a wind-burn night.

You must see, she tells. She pulls me. She pushes. She carries me.

Charbonneau grit-eyes me like an old Goose and then waves me away.

Come, Corn Necklace says. Come now.

We make our way through camp bustle. People dance. People prepare for Buffalo. Smoke rises from their heat.

Corn Necklace hides her face beneath her robe hood. We pass traders and bargain Hunters, whoops, squeals, smoke fires, foot games, fat hiss. We come to where Village opens into a wide circle. There is beautiful Song, heart Song, drumming. *Spirit* flags flap over Lodges. My heart pounds. Only People who own *Medicine Bundles* live in the circle and face the Sacred Cedar.

Men with young Wives stand beside the great Lodge. The Lodge is lit with crack and roar of fire. Monster shadows darken skin walls where the Ancient Ones gather.

Women heft their robes and bulk themselves against Husband shoulder bumps.

Before Women enter the Lodge, their eyes squiddle like mice in Hawk talons.

Corn Necklace points her mouth as the Lodge flap opens. Smoke haze.

I squint. I do not see what I see. I cannot.

I see traders who Women-joke and Women-barter. White men who size us like Beaver pelts. We are short or ugly, small-mouthed or plain. We are dark or light. We are fat or thin or pretty or pug-faced. We are Goose fat or stink waddle.

Wide-eyed ugly white men watch what I cannot see. They watch *must-not-be-named*. They buck with silent laughter. They snort. They hiss. They piss their selves. They do not take their eyes from their watching—they gadder like War men. No, not War men, like boys who hunt Turtles .. threaded to their looking .. eyes locked.

I move closer.

Lewis stands beside Clark. All his men squint through fire smoke and gawk at *must-not-be-named*. Black Man shields his eyes and smalls his self like the naked Women in the circle.

I curl my arms around my swollen belly. One man removes his wife's robe. I see the standing points of her nipples before she closes her shoulders and folds in on herself .. shame shame shame shame before white men's boil-pot laughter.

A Death-push witters from bulge-loins of white men watching .. Their smell—revolts from mouse nests and poisoned mouths, a stench stronger than musk-marrow desiccating in creek beds—is the same smell Onion Wife found when she found White Crow broken. White men finger their Holy Metals while their cocks rise. White men and their Devil stand before
must-not-be-named ..

I am sick. My body festers with these slittering snuckling Devil men worse than War men. These Women barterers infesting our Rivers and grasses, infesting our Mountains and Streams—infesting and in-fester-ing *the Sacred*. They are Wolves of men. Traders of Bear skins and kettle pots, tatter pelts and Women.

I can look no more.

Days of honor

I go to sweat.

I enter cold River to wash myself. To clean myself.

I pray.

I Smudge. I ask Sweetgrass to enter my lungs, my heart, my liver, to carry my prayers.

I pray *the Wise One* protects my child.

I thank Earth.

I thank the four directions.

I ask to be cleansed. I ask to be cleansed. I ask to be cleansed. I ask to be cleansed.

Days of white men dancing

White men sing as they leave the Fort to scuffer other men's wives. Meat Scrape stands guard outside his Lodge while York forn-i-cates his wife.

York is Lewis and Clark's Medicine boat launch, greater than the Great White Father. His loins more powerful than the white men's guns, more potent than their glinting President metals.

Clark parades York like big shining Horse, Horse more beautiful than other Horses. When Women chase York, when Warriors glint-eye York, Clark flinch-steps.

Clark knows the People see only York, not white man's guns, not white man's uniforms or metals, not his Corn grinders or blacksmith. Not Clark.

For punishment for his beauty, Clark takes away York's Buffalo robe, feeds him less than other men. Feeds him less than Hidatsa Horse.

Clark thumps York's belly like a gourd. Lose weight, Clark tells York. You are not nearly as fit as I am. You shame me.

of cunt stink

Broke Leg brings Many Teeth to Sergeant Ordway. Broke Leg struts and jigs when he shows his favor wife to Glug Glug. He wants Glug Glug to want what he has.

The People call Sergeant Ordway Glug Glug because he swallows and swallows before and after he talks. He swallows whenever he is spoken to. His Glug Glug eyes are blink blink eyes round and empty as a baby who will not learn. Crazy carrot speckled yellow root eyes, blue as white men veins.

Glug Glug swallows then swallows again like he will eat Many Teeth, like she is green Buffalo melt.

Beautiful Many Teeth.

Glug Glug does not deserve her fullness, her jiggly warm arms, her Mother teats, her wide baby-carry shoulders. Her sex.

When white men talk sex, he swallows. Glug Glug. He gawks. Glug Glug. Blink Blink.

Glug Glug strips to bare butt before he enters Broke Leg's branch Lodge for fornication.

For long night, Many Teeth screams and whistles and spills out hut with Glug Glug sucking. Rubbing. Licking her axe chop. Glug Glug all night long.

of long business

Charbonneau must speak to Clark about his situation. It is urgent! Charbonneau says. He has changed his mind. He will go. We will go.

We sit in Clark's hot cabin while Clark finishes business.

Clark sits at his big desk. Only York can touch Clark's big desk, and only when he wrestles big desk from boat, up bank, across camp to Fort. And then day after day whenever Clark wants his big desk moved to the porch outside, or back inside, beside fire, away from fire. It is of utmost importance that no one speak while Clark is at his desk. It is verboten. No one bothers Clark when he sits at his big desk. No one but Charbonneau.

I tire of Clark's scribble pen .. scratch-scribble scratch-scribble.

We are *ghosts* in Clark's candlelit room. He talks to his self as he writes.

Old Goose's head drops to his chest . . . snaw . . . snahh . . . snaw . . . snaw. But when Clark begins talking, when he starts to read the words he has written, I sit up. I pay attention like |He is woman| and Appe taught me. I miss no word. I hear every tongue tap. I remember. I commit.

Dear Julia, Clark whispers, and then reads aloud.

No no.

My dearest Julia, *A tad bit better. Yes.*

My station at Fort Mandan would try the souls of good men. At times, I share a small room with some rascally characters.

No no. That will never do. Uh, well then. Perhaps.

My dear dear Julia

It has been months since I beheld your face.

Memories of you are like sun rays through these dark November clouds.

He sighs and pats his head and then scribble-scratches some more. He smashes his paper and then picks it up again. He sighs and reaches for new paper sheet.

Dear Brother, he says, and taps his feather in ink.

I listen for River moving and creaking and think of Blue Elk.

I understand what white men say now.

Clark calls me Janey. *I once knew a lovely girl named Jane. Her laughter was infectious. I don't suppose you would mind if I called you Janey.*

I smile and look at him with blind eyes when he calls me Janey. I wish White Man and |He is woman| had not taught me to understand English.

Appe, why did you ask me to listen to White Man?

I wish |He is woman| had never asked me to remember, to recollect, to one day write down every word the white men said. I hear their words in my sleep. I startle awake hoping I have not given myself away. I must hide what I know. No Woman can live with the knowledge of all white War men say.

I tire of doors, Fort barricades, and white men's stingy-gut ways to own all things and keep all things to their selves.

|He is woman| says white men believe we did not live before they came. Crazy white men to think they created us. Crazy Indians to want what white men offer. They offer nothing.

Outside their doors and their barricades, we disappear.

Jessaume enters and cold air whooshes behind him.

Charbonneau snorts awake, and talk passes from Charbonneau to Jessaume to Clark, and then back.

Men hunt, complain, or fornicate. Gadder gadder gadder of grump. White men talk.

I push myself to stand and River to the door. Charbonneau does not think I will run pregnant.

He waves me off with his hand.

Night air swells and opens, and I run.

of pummel women

Otter Woman and I gather driftwood. We build a great fire
and stand near. We drink hot bitter coffee and visit. Wind skitters
through Mandan. It is so cold we wrap in Buffalo robes and line our
moccasins with Cattail fluff and Rabbit fur.

You're not big, Otter Woman says, and rubs my belly. I will
make you Buffalo marrow and bitter greens. I will make you thick
black Juniper tea.

We have not seen Buffalo for days. The People fear Buffalo will
not return.

Otter Woman whispers stories. She wishes to live with Alive
Beside Arrow. She wishes to have his babies. She wishes to leave
Man-who-plagues-us.

Clark says it is twenty below.

It is the Season babies freeze in Mothers' Wombs.

Snow squeaks like a white man's saddle beneath our feet.

Thin Moon cuts Sky. We throw wood on the fire. We close in
together and see into flames.

Does Clark see twenty white men below River ice? Down
down down down where Mandan once lived?

Will spring come when the last white men surface from the
dark below?

We hear high laughter. Devil titter. Coyote laugh.

Laugh-cry.

Smell rises from camp. Mouse sniff. Blacksmith clink. Blood
lick from a white man's knife.

Animal scudders past .. My scalp tingles.

Corn Necklace calls out to us from darkness. My Sister. My
Sister, she shouts.

Many Teeth walks slowly beside Corn Necklace. She limps, cradles her ribs, and then stops. She steps again so slowly she moves little. Her head steams like boil pots. Her face rains sweat. I smell sting-blood. Copper kettle stench. I go to her.

Corn Necklace and I hold up Many Teeth but as we walk I feel hot-wet soak my side. I look behind and see blood trail.

I send Otter Woman for Clark and for blankets and she returns with Clark's Medicine Bag.

We sit Many Teeth down by fire. She hisses with pain. Her jaw is spoiling meat. Black. Raccoon-black. Blood-settle black. She becomes old Horse with Rattler-bitten face. Her chest bruised the color of smoke suns.

My Husband beat me, she chatters, through broken teeth. He stabbed me so many times I cry for my children.

We pack her wounds. Her eyes flitter white. All Around her blood darkens snow.

Man smitters and sneaks toward us like we are Deer herd. Hard snow cricks beneath his footsteps. Broke Leg cannot slink on anyone.

Corn Necklace stands to shield Many Teeth. We roar at him. We lurch at him. We kick.

My robe staggers heat. I flame so hot I can melt more snows than fires.

Otter Woman grabs long driftwood and beats Broke Leg. We surround him screaming. We push him. We grab his knife. He cannot get past us. He whimpers like a baby.

Clark hears the commotion. He is too late. We have driven Broke Leg back to darkness.

We will chase him from our Lodge, Corn Necklace says. We will scratch him with poison arrows. We will tie him up with Elk rope and drag him to River. We will whip him like a dog.

Clark backs away from us. He understands our language now.
Yes, Corn Necklace, tells him. You should go or we take you. You
brought this to our Women. You brought ugly Men to our camp.
Fire hisses and wood drops into a hundred sparks.

of men and Men

Glug Glug stands behind barricade. He is the white man who causes Many Teeth trouble. He peers out like a Weasel looking for Turtle eggs. He has his big guns and his fort. He has men who will protect him.

Coward, Otter Woman says.

Many Teeth suffers through the ice-slivered night, her lungs puffing clouds, her body spilling blood and water. She is butcher-mouthed, guttering with first light.

Debai-yellow Sky shivers. Cold needles our skin.

All night we doctor Many Teeth. Many Teeth lives to see morning.

Beautiful Rider appears on the high bluff. Snow unfurls in sparkling clouds behind *His* running Horse. Fearless Man. Horse brays, slides, and Rider kicks, then kicks again.

Horse chuffs and charges us and |He is man| reins up and swoops Meriwether off Horse's back.

Many Teeth's blood startles snow All Around .. All Around us. But it is no matter to Meriwether. He sees only his self.

Meriwether Lewis. Captain Lewis. Narrow-shouldered big man speaks to no one. Out hunting. Puh. Three days gone. |He is woman| knew. *He comes with shame. He comes with anger. He comes with sodomy.*

The barricade gate shudders and squeals as it closes behind him. |He is man| lifts Many Teeth up on *His* Horse.

Days of lung crackle

Clark says the mercury stands at forty below.
My teats ache with cold.
My baby kicks to keep us both warm.
I huddle over my belly like it is fire that will go out.

Days of endless counting and cataloging

We live in Lewis and Clark's Lodge. Charbonneau says he is an important interpreter and guide to important men.

Lewis whispers as he counts his loot. He whispers on and on and writes down everything he sees, everything he and his white men kill and collect.

1 & 2 skins of the Male and female Antelope with their skeletons. & the Skin of a Yellow Bear/Specimens of plants numbered 1-60/Earthen pot Such as the Mandans manufacture and use for culinary purposes.

Water spill-splashes my legs .. my feet ..

White men circle like Wolves that lick their dry black lips. They force me to lie down, to open my legs to them.

I do not want to birth baby in white man camp. I hold my bowels. I fight my Womb pulse. I boulder my legs.

I want my Sister, I yell. I want Otter Woman. But Charbonneau does not send for her. He does not want her trouble.

I hold back until I can fight no longer.

Birthing goes on into night and longer night. I push and push and my Womb hole gapes. I want to stand.

I am ripe plum split. I am oversweet with birth. I am shitting rot.

White men watch like I am Ceremony, like I am Dance. They speak like I cannot hear.

I hear squirrel sleep, mouse quake, batwing flutter.

This is her first child, Clark says. It is customary for it to take a long time, but I fear her hips are too narrow.

Lewis links his hands at the back of his neck. First child, he says, born to a child. Let's hope she survives. How old do you think she is? Lewis asks.

Young, Clark answers, younger than my Julia.

And how old is dear Julia? Lewis asks.

She was twelve when I left Virginia.

Long time ago, at Three Forks, a Woman died in childbirth. Baby-blue ice spat from her cold Womb. Am I to be split open by white man's baby?

A white man forces my mouth open. I fight. Clark presses Rattler tail down my throat. I cannot swallow. I cannot breathe.

Am I to die in childbirth? My Womb is heavy. My robe is blood soaked. I am tired. I am so tired. Light glitters on silver River. Agai leap and their red bodies become the color of my sleep.

It's time to Walk with Buffalo, Old Woman says. Come with me.

I do not want to be taken to Sacred Lodge like Corn Necklace. I do not wish to be laughed at by white men and forced to fornicate with any man they choose.

Do not worry, Old Woman says. No harm will come to you.

I am losing breath. I am turning to ice.

Young Daughter. Old Woman taps my shoulder. Life is here, she says. She rubs my chest and sings and her Song is so sweet it lifts me. I sleep with Juniper.

To Walk with Buffalo is to touch the center of the pulsing universe, to become one with Life itself. You will see.

Poor men believe other men's power will pass to them through Women's vaginas. How could they not? Women are powerful. Ah, but wise men have always known Women's center heart. Women's Womb is mightier than any War party. The true path to power is through the vagina.

Vagina?

Vagina, she says, a good word. Other words you've heard white men speak, are not. If you did not understand his words you would still understand brute meaning.

In my sweat bath I moan. Someone has axed me. Axed me all the way from my ass to my cunt. I am split open. I am roaring with Life and with Death.

Axe chop! She splutters. White Men and their senseless ways!

She points at her crotch. Life, she says. Not violence. Ever.

Her mirrors glitter and glitter and Bia takes up every shine. One hundred mirrors become Bia reaching for me.

It is your time, Bia says.

I hear crying. My baby.

Jean Baptiste, Charbonneau says.

Welcome, Baptiste, the white men say, lifting alcohol to their lips. Cheers!

Every day begins

with a recitation of all the things the white men are taking.
Buffalo robe painted by Mandan man representing a battle fought 8
years Since by the Sioux and Recaras against the mandans
No. 12. The bones & Skeleton of a Small burrowing wolf of the Prairies
the Skin being lost by accedent.

Sergeant Ordway dresses in finest regalia and Clark parades him like mightiest warrior. York trails behind.

The People do not care to see Glug Glug. They give all eyes to York.

Glug Glug gives Broke Leg a red scarf, blue beads, a tin pipe.

No one touched your squaw except this man, Clark says, and pat-pats Glug Glug's shoulder like a proud Appe. You, he says eyeing Broke Leg, gave Sergeant Ordway use of her for the night. He winks at Broke Leg.

Clark turns and spreads his arms to the Grand Chief and the People. No man of my party shall touch another man's squaw.

Broke Leg's jealousy bubbles his belly like maggots. Broke Leg captures his own hands in his armpits. His knees shake. Clark does not see meanness. He only sees his self talking, making gestures.

Clark tells the People he stopped Broke Leg from an unfortunate act. As your wife, you could have lawfully killed her, he tells Broke Leg, but I prevented any murder from taking place.

He lies.

Take your squaw home, Clark says. Live happily together.

Days of budding Moon

Warm days come with sour berries, skulls and skeletons, fuming carcasses of Buffalo.

All Around great boil pots roil. They feast on soup the color of white man's green bottles. Good smells of green smoke drift from Villages.

Putrid, the Traders say, holding their noses. But the smell is like alcohol that becomes sweeter in the mouth.

Charbonneau has many tasks for me. I gather driftwood to heat his bones even as the days turn warm. He cooks wood squirrels and dried cherries with sage and Juniper berries, a thick stew he eats slowly.

Jean Baptiste is a fat baby at my breast.

When I pass Lewis and Clark's Lodge they are hunched over reading.

No. 11 a Martin Skin, Containing the tail of a Mule Deer, a weasel and three Squirels from the Rockey mountains.

Now I leave Mandan Camp

Lewis counts inventory. He counts all his possessions and all he will take.

Box No. 1, contains the following articles i. e.

In package No. 3 & 4 Male & female antelope, with their Skelitions. No. 7 & 9 the horns of two mule or Black tailed deer, a Mandan bow and quiver of arrows—with some Recara's tobacco seed.

I am the article Charbonneau will take. I keep lookout for Lost His Head to Horse but he does not chase through grasses or jump at me.

Corn Grease walks long path to offer gifts. She gives me Corn knife she made. She gives me gristle chew for baby. She sniffles and pat-pats my shoulders. You will be my Sister, she says.

I am injured by her tremble gut, her petting.

Too Ott Lok stands in quiet and my eyes become heavy. Water spills down my cheeks. Blue Elk waits. You go home now, he says. I will send you a gift. Remember.

I will see your Bia, I say, but can say no more.

Tell her my name is Walks Many Ways now, Too Ott Lok says.

Otter Woman sits beside me and holds Jean Baptiste. She squeezes my leg. She does not let go until the Captains are ready. She gives me her digging stick. It can be used many ways, she says. Do not let Man-who-plagues-us harm you.

Corn Necklace grips my hand. My liver twists to leave her with Broke Leg.

Boats launch

The People come to watch us leave. We pass them in silence.

Debai is pale fizz in Sky, so bright my eyes ache.

Old Goose, Droulliard, and York ride in Clark's white boat. I small myself at the back. Clark sits in shade and hums. The white men are giddy to leave. They dance around each other. They sing to themselves.

Lewis walks the bank holding a line to our boat. He walks like Warrior off to chase Buffalo.

Jean Baptiste cries and wind carries his cry to Mandan. On the low bluff a Man runs behind a Woman running. The Woman calls to us. She cries to us. I will be your Wife for Dark Nights, she calls to Men rowing, to Men moving on. Take me with you.

As we pass I see it is Many Teeth. She drops to her knees in front of Lewis.

Her Brother catches her. Take her with you, he pleads.

Lewis holds up his hands like she is his jumping dog. I hear snatches of her talk. Her Brother's crumbled voice. And then their voices fade as white men press on, as their oars catch Water, catch Water.

I look for |He is man|He is woman|He is now Many| but not *One* comes.

But the Beautiful Women are running, running the banks of the black spring River, waving, calling. The white men are laughing.

York weeps, wheezes, hides his face.

The white men jostle each other—mistake-believe they are desirable.

No. 99 The Skeliton of the white and Grey hare.

Day of going on

When we pull to shore, I work alone. Men spy me from bushes. Watch me when I shit. Eye my nurse teats.

Scrittering mice take pity on me and uncover their sweet root stash.

We set up camp near Water falls. In the glower Moon, in the dark surround, Water falls over black rocks become white skeletons.

When I squat in the bushes, I hear someone moving in Trees. I stop and clutch a rock to my chest.

I hear bracelets shake. I listen. Bracelets, jickle of shells.

I see you are happy to see me, *She* says. Do not worry, Little Storm. When you have taught someone, you never leave them.

Know I will be here, *She* says and taps my forehead.

When I turn *She* is gone.

Stutter of days

Surrounded by white men, my world becomes small. I have no stories to tell. My only story is survival.

We enter roses where *White Buffalo* thread clumps of their own *Sacred* hair among the thorns. Lewis fingers the *thing-not-to-be-touched* and believes it to be only sun-faded.

What you know to be Beautiful is Ugly. You will see blood traces of the Dead on rose thorns where you gather food.

I could sell this magnificent hair, Lewis says. Must be five pounds of wool. What do you suppose I could get for it? he asks. Surely, it would fetch a handsome sum.

I pray as I walk *what-should-not-be-walked*. I cover my baby's head. Lewis heads off into silence talking to himself.

What matter? if the waters sleep
In silence and obscurity.

Two men fight over a fat Beaver. They stake the World they see.

When Lewis returns, he tells us he has something to announce. I have discovered forty-three temporary Indian Lodges, he says.

He is blind. No People stay here. He pokes old camp rings where the Dead are hidden.

Days of into on

The day is bleached as the Buffalo skulls we pass. Dead Buffalo stack River so deep Wolves stagger under the weight of their own wobbly bellies. Lazy Wolves lay beside Buffalo and gnaw on green melt flesh.

Lewis gutters laughter as he walks up to meat-swollen Wolf and shoots.

We are entering *Lone Man's* place where we find only things *Coyote* left behind. Hills burned black as caldrons. Deep Earth hissing at *edges-of-dark*. Woods where no one stops.

We scare awake by a blazing Tree. Of all the Trees in the Forest only this Tree torches, flaming over the Lodge where the Captains sleep. The fiery tree top plummets down on our tent and blitzes into a thousand tiny sparks, a floor of fire.

Clark calls the fire the Devil's fire and the men pull their tents closer together but no one, not even Lewis, sleeps.

Whooter, weehoo sounds breeze through the high Tree tops. Flickers of lights bleat near River. Woohoop. Woohoop.

Cruzatte's fiddle plays in the dark, and then quiets, and we all tilt our heads to listen.

Someone is beating a hand drum .. beyond River .. Crosses River .. Circles camp.

It is nothing, Lewis says. It is a branch hitting a hollow log.

Only Lewis says we are superstitious, frightened like children. Cruzatte sits in silence by the campfire, his fiddle tucked in his knapsack, while the sound of his music wheedles through the Trees.

Days of plunder

We have walked and walked through mud and dust and sludge Water. Up hillsides, along creek Waters, beside hush Land where nothing moves but Prairie dogs. Prairie dogs peek out of their holes, ring their round tails, round and round. Chit chit to each other. And all the Prairie dogs move together up and down leaping like fleas. Chatting to each other. Charting us. Warning each other the white men are here.

Men split up and go off to scout, to hunt, to have time alone. Some men disappear for days and return carrying haunches of venison, belts of Rabbit meat. Lewis takes out his instruments and peers down a long metal tube. Men measure, and map, and chipmunk the Land. They tromp Burial sites where Death odors skitter from rocks.

Through shade grasses, up hillsides, and down deep grassy troughs, I hear clicking, high whistles, wheezing. When I stop Charbonneau pushes me forward. But when I fuss with Jean Baptiste, when I lag and catch up, I see *Weta* watching.

In midday when we have rocked in boat swells and heat fries the stink of sugar lead medicine, the sweet, sweet tinny odor of white men bolts from powder blister feet, blister backs, blister hands.

I cannot eat from the stench.

Days of carrying

I rub my teats with gray bark powder, and after suck, I pat
his back, but Jean Baptiste cannot shit. Jean Baptiste is heavy in
my arms. Heavy on my kidneys, kicking, kicking, kicking. He is
Buffalo leg. All day carry weight. No Sister help. No Husband help.
White man's baby is a thump-thumping Jack Rabbit. Nothing but
kick in my arms . .   When I look at him, I see Charbonneau's
face drip over me. My back bows under Charbonneau's weight. I
do not want this baby. I want him to float away in River gurgle.
Puh. I am tired of washing shit cloths, tired of wiping spit up.
Teeth butcher his gums. He will not stop crying. I pat and pat
him. He shits. He soils me. I wash his butt. Stream Water is so
cold he screams.

I look for pesky men who wish to split me, and when I see I am
alone, I cry with baby.

Black Man does not see me at first. He stares into dark woods
with jiggly eyes.

I want to be alone. I want to be alone. Men. Pester men.

I pat my face. No man will see me cry.

Black Man is quiet for a long while. I jiggle Jean Baptiste to
settle him. I rub his gums.

York begins to speak his Life to the woods, his voice a chitter light, his words a spidery sinew that catches Bird commotion in
Trees, squirrels stop their chit chit chit chatter. Deer still. Ogres roll
again in wind tumble waves. *Spirits* whistle low.

He speaks in a low whisper-gutter that wobbles.

I listen with all of me. His story howls along my spine, yelps
my liver.

I cover Jean Baptiste's head. Some stories come from rot belly.
York's story quivers with Death spew. I feel its spray before he tells it.

Willie is Master Clark, he says, to me. I bet you didn't know that. Yes, Mam, he calls himself Master.

I look at Jean Baptiste's toes. I am busy. I show him I do not understand his words but York talks to me. He goes on.

I grew up with him. We were the same age at one time. But when you're a man's slave, years eat you. I was bequeathed to him. Bequeathed, given away by Death to a spoiled child. Can you imagine? I know you can.

I was almost twelve years old when Old Mister, that's Clark's father, insisted I accompany Willie to the circus.

I'd have to hunker down, Old Mister said. Stay out of everybody's way. I was only there to serve. The old man told me I'd get whipped if I cracked a smile.

I didn't let on that I wanted to go. I'd heard about the circus. Clowns and acrobats and tightrope walkers and beautiful white women in glittery costumes spraying fire from their mouths. Incomprehensible! A magnificent display of god-defying acts. A sight for whites only and maybe a few poop sweeps.

I felt I was the luckiest damn kid. The circus was in town and I was going.

But we didn't go to any circus. I wasn't even taken off the property. Old Mister led me to a section of his place out back in the woods. Willie was sniggering the whole time but I wasn't worried until I saw men standing beside this big old shack—waiting for Old Mister to let them in. They had this look on their faces. A shameful look. A murderous stare.

Old Mister forced me to disrobe down to bare naked. I tried to hide myself but he had me get up on a stump where everyone could see.

For a long while there was quiet. Old Mister held his lamplight up to me with these men looking on and Willie trying to hold back laughter while I flinched from the burn of kerosene spit.

I became aware of somebody close. Huffing in the darkness behind me. Chains clinking, rattling.

A whoop-stink of Death.

I'd never had a girl before let alone a woman. All these ogling white men, poking fun, laughing, stink-eyeing us. Jeering us to copulate. Trying to see what they should not be seeing. Something both foul and sacred.

Old Mister took his belt off and I felt the sting of his leather on my ass. Get to it, he yelled.

Her woman insides burned hot as a caldron. I never felt heat like that. A sulfur in me. As the lantern swung and as I inhaled her bone-Death scent, I saw her lizard eyes flicker with tiny skitters of Lightning.

She was a witch. A real witch.

Those men didn't know what hit 'em. They got hexed that night. They shoulda known. I don't know how they couldn't see it coming. I guess white folks have a hard time believing there's more to the world than a white man in the heavens. They don't believe in real witches even when one is looking at them.

The oglers brought the hex home with them too. They thought all the sudden Deaths were just natural causes.

But I knew.

Now I *know you know something* these white men don't know. And you wouldn't tell no one because there's no good person to trust.

But something isn't right. There's the same feeling here that hummed in that shack. Something in the air here like devil powder.

You feel it too. Don't you? We're seeing things we shouldn't be seeing.

I do not look at York as I wrap Jean Baptiste and head back to camp.

Lewis asks Charbonneau to man the boat while he scouts the River bank. And then Lewis disappears. Tall grasses shither. Debai tatters Water.

Charbonneau lights his pipe. He is not one to steer anything. He gawks around. He leans back on my knees. But now is quiet. He cannot bring his trouble. Charbonneau points to a shimmering Tree. In its branches is a giant Magpie nest. Red-Winged Blackbirds call from reeds. An Otter bloops beneath Water, and then reappears beside us—looking, watching, pawing. Jean Baptiste flaps his arms and gurgles.

Up ahead, Cruzatte pays attention. He stands to steer his pirogue. Debai flitters behind a scatter of clouds.

In the not-far-away, clouds scutter. And then clouds move in.

I feel a chill breeze. A press of wind at my back. And then grit wind sings around my face. River wrinkles. Cold moans over the creaking boat.

I wrap Jean Baptiste and strap him back in his cradleboard. I make sure he is cinched to me.

Wind shrieks and River crickles, and turns, and moves faster and faster and waves as high as my waist crash over the lip of the boat.

Wind whistles, whips high Water over Charbonneau. Over me.

Charbonneau cannot swim, cannot steer, cannot paw Water. He honks and splutters and becomes Old Goose again. He cries to god. Waves slop over his head and he screams. Jean Baptiste squeals.

Black wood boxes float out of the ship and Charbonneau latches on to me like he will float away.

I scoop Water and look for Lewis to help. Clark runs beside us and yells to us from River bank. Clark tells Charbonneau to clip the sail.

Lewis clashes through the watery grass along River bank. Oh, my god, he says, my instruments. Get the boxes! Grab the goddamn boxes!

Charbonneau's lower lip quivers with slobber.

Scoop out Water, I tell Charbonneau. Scoop.

I lean over and pull the boxes back into the boat.

Charbonneau splashes Water like a baby.

A breeze wheezes around us. There is change. *Transformation.*

Someone moves

                     Beyond the clearing

Moves

        Through leaves and tall spring grasses.

Moves

               Over low hillsides.

Someone follows us.

Jean Baptiste whimpers and whines and Clark sings to him from River line.

Froggy went a courtin' and he did ride, uh-huh

A shimmer of stink welters up from the banks .. smattering crunching crackling.

Pomp went a courtin' and he did ride, uh-huh

I know not to lift my head ..

A Tree .. not a Tree .. taller than Moose .. crashes through brush and Trees .. spits twigs, seedpods. Wind shears saplings and twists Corn sheaths upward where no Corn sheaths grow.

I see arms .. a head that is not a head. Grasses whine, and the Corn stalk, and the wood grass, and the orange bramble become a Woman mightier than this army—twirling twirling twirling twirling.

Look, I whisper. I keep my head low so only Earth hears me, A *Wood Spirit*.

I fold my arms back over my baby.

Wood Spirit buzzes with a sound like sap splintering wood stands in a frozen lake.

Lewis cups his hands to his throat and coughs.

York's eyes open wide and he runs beside us.

Men oar with might but we move little. Wind whitens River ..

Wind wind wind wind wind wind wind wind wind wind wind wind wind wind wind wind wind

wind wind wind wind .. Charbonneau loses the sail and the boat pitches on its side. Waves splash over us a second time, a third time. I cradle Jean Baptiste and pull boxes back into boat .. my hair a blizzard.

Charbonneau becomes Old Goose, honks again, and cries.

And as *Spirit* passes I pray for safe passage. I pray for Jean Baptiste. I pray for the White Cliffs up ahead, and the Birds that swirl round them. I pray for River.

Our boats cut voices *we-should-not-hear* and splits *Spirit* currents.

White men whimper but do not speak of such things. These men do not pray, do not thank *Spirits* for passage.

Day of heartsick men

Pierre fiddles by the fire. He plays so sweetly River sings. Earth coos.

This trek, this hard foot walk.

Lewis sits by River. His tear-shiny face. His lips pink as dusk smudged by fire.

Clark sits beside quiet Lewis and juggles Pomp on his leg.

To market, to market to buy a fat pig.

Home again, home again

Jiggedy jig.

Day of no-good alone

Men follow me everywhere.

Charbonneau meets Lewis's men away from camp. Out of sight of Lewis and Clark, he hunkers in bushes with these War men and Hunters and returns with treasures: a goat pouch of wine, a clunky emerald ring, a sack full of trade beads and musket balls.

Men no longer peek at me. They are bold as Crows. They peck at me. Gawk at me. They close in on me and sniff. They fumble for my cunt if I pass too close. When I feed Jean Baptiste, they rub their swelled cocks.

I clench wedge rocks in my fists, make knives from splinter Trees and sharpen them in fire until they can slice knuckle bones. I hide them where I squat.

May I have a word with you, Captain Clark? Lewis asks. Will you excuse us, Men?

Lewis Wolf-eyes his men and they skulk to other chores.

York keeps his head down, his eyes down, his shoulders down. He makes sure supplies are dry, clean. He works when others stop. He heaves heavy kegs from boats every day, every night. He empties boats filled with Water while Clark tells him to empty boats filled with Water. What York hears is little nothing to Clark.

Christ, Charbonneau has the balls of a Buffalo, Lewis says.

I listen.

Clark rubs Rabbit brush between his palms, listens, his eyebrows pinched.

Lewis calls York over. They keep their gadder voices low.

They look my way.

Clark places his hand on York's shoulder and squeezes.

That's your job now, York, Clark says, when he lets go.

York shades his eyes and looks at me. His mouth bends upward. He is not smiling.

When I wash Jean Baptiste, York is there. When I squat to shit, York turns his back. When I take Jean Baptiste to my teat, York waits. When Jean Baptiste cries, York listens.

In the blackest night when Moon is cloud covered and animals still, York rises to watch me piss, to watch me walk Jean Baptiste, to watch me.

She has her own goddamn sentinel, the men say, their eyes fizzing, their smell as sour as hoof rot.

I pinch York's wrist when he reaches for bowls of marrow bones peppered with stinging cress. Some men shit. Some blister. Some drip puss that shimmers like mercury. Most cannot eat for days.

Would I feel safe if I did not understand? Would their words still butcher me?

I point to Elk spleen, and Clark gives it to me with a smile. I gather ants in my Water pouch and leave them in Debai until they dry to powder. On a hot rock, I decay spleen, and when it withers, I pound ants and spleen together to make a dark sticky dust that can poison any man, any animal.

I can kill the Devil.

Days of Woman ache and throb

Now we must sleep in the skin hut with Clark and Lewis and Charbonneau. It is difficult to call him Charbonneau. He is only Stink to me now.

At night, Stink climbs on top of me and huffs. His cock in me is dry Deer bone. Rock rattles. Hurt and hurt. His melt like scat.

I tighten my cunt to make him spill. He is loud in his grunt-huff. He wants whole camp to hear him. To hear his fornication. To hear he is with Woman. They catch what Stink offers like disease, like quiet pox. Men wake and listen. I hear the thrum-throb of their cocks. I hear their fast breath calls to each other.

I moan sometimes to get out of my gut, out of my skin, out from under Stink. Mistake. Men think I enjoy myself.

Clark is so quiet the roots of his hair catch fire.

Day of Sergeant Gas

Days hack at me. Sounds of guns. Sounds of animals dying. Animals crying in animal traps.

I pull Jean Baptiste's blanket over both our heads. I hold my hands over my ears.

Sergeant Gas watches me. He is an old Waddle-puss. Pzzzt.

He old man pisses. He cannot hold back his sour wind pzzzt pzzst. He scribbles. He watches. He pzzzt.

He shows me a sketch he has drawn of me, and when I look he pulls it from my hands and wads it up in his fists.

Day to stop for men watch

I want to jump from the boat and run. I want to be away from men. Appe was wrong. There are no stories in crazy.

Men lift their oars and pole the boats so they can stop and ogle, so they can giggle and gadder.

They watch. Eyes fixed. Mouths open. They slap each other. Whistle.

Bears copulate. Bears fuck and roar. Their great muscles shiver. White men watch, with their cocks like Lightning rods, like a dog with pink stick.

At night Lewis and Clark and others read all the things they have gathered.

The party killed two Elk and a Buffaloe today, and my dog caught a goat, which he overtook by superior fleetness, the goat must be understood was young and extremely poor.

Day of poor ways

Seaman snarls, slobber-drools over pitiful Goat scraps.
Dog growls at Pomp chewing gristle. Clark slaps him away.

Days Clark talks

Oh my dear Janey, I must tell you about the sea. I know you couldn't possibly understand but I feel it is my great calling to sing its wonder.

There are Fish bigger than the largest Buffalo, he says. Waves bigger than hills. Waves that go on and on. Water so vast, so immense you cannot see the other side.

I will take you to the oceanside, Janey. We will breathe in the good salty air. We will build castles in the sand. We will watch the great whales leap and spout their mighty breaths.

I have fished the great waters. I have reeled in Fish bigger than any man.

If there is magic in this World, we will find it together, my dear, in the great waters of the seas.

Days of York's enslavement

Clark leads York to Lewis and Lewis leads York into the shadow woods.

The men are ordered to stay. They glint-eye each other, crack side-smiles, giggle into their chests.

Lewis's dog bites and yaps at his tether, leaps forward, wants to follow.

On still days we hear Lewis in those woods, over that hill, in the hidden Canyons. We hear his pant, his gleeful puffs, his laughing wa-wa-wail.

The men grimace when they return.

York covers his face and Lewis struts like a man who has eaten Buffalo strap.

I watch York. I cannot look away. Days are measured by his misery.

Pierre pulls out his fiddle and the men drink and jig but do not look beyond firelight where York mourns himself in darkness.

Weta's shadow drops over me and over the tent where I sleep. *Weta's* shadow Monsters the men. Clark pants awake. Lewis whimpers. Charbonneau curls in on his self.

In the dark Corn rows we sit knee to knee.

Did you know, |He is woman|, says, Black Man has to accompany Lewis whenever he visits Many Spirit?

Poor Black Man has no interest in visiting our Lodge. He has his own Medicine.

No good will come to Captain Lewis. He carries his shame like a Rabbit stole, alive and whimpering, around his shoulders. I can see him. Up ahead.

A Black Woman will leave him to die.

Up ahead? I ask.

Yes, |He is woman| says. Up ahead, where Meriwether lifts a musket to his head and his head cracks like a Spruce feather. Up ahead where Meriwether slashes his own throat with goat shears.

Day of gifts that are not gifts

Clark hands me a long white strip. A ribbon of lace for you, he says.

You want beautiful things for your son, don't you? Pretty things fit for a king? I can give Pomp an education, a fine house, music, books, travel.

Lewis pats his shoulder. Valiant effort, Captain. But she's a savage squaw. She doesn't understand a word you say. You could offer her a pot of gold and she'd prefer a bouquet of weeds or to gnaw on a putrid Buffalo leg.

They laugh.

Clark breathes in Jean Baptiste's hair while Jean Baptiste sucks my teat. Sweet baby, Pomp, Clark says. Sweet, sweet baby.

Days of trap for the Great White Father

Lewis and Clark are sending Fox to the Great White Father. They do not know they have trapped *Spirit Fox*, who carries the weight of a man possessed by *must-not-be-named*.

Meriwether places caged *Fox* at the edge of camp because *His* cage is foul as pig's blood, he says. But I know Meriwether is afraid.

Every night caged *Fox* moves when night fastens the Moon-heavy Water to *Spirits*,
when light sifts down through dark currents and River begins chanting.

Do not look, I want to warn them, there at the bottom, there along the lip of shore where

Water channels *must-not-be-named*. Do white men know the dim Sky Water carries is older than time, older than blood .. bigger. I cannot save these men from what comes. I cannot save myself. I pray for Pomp. I pray for River. I pray for *Fox*.

In the deepest still place of River, *Fox* is chanting. *Fox* conjures Death—Beaver-slick currents to overturn boats. A fool's beauty. Sparkling scales of Fish scatter silt.

Fox gnashes his teeth. *His* black mouth snaps at *His* cage, *His* teeth bite/bite/bite/bite. Clark can't put *His* cage far enough away from me.

In the dark *He* is the thing moving. I wake to *His* rattling cage beside me. *Fox* whispers a harsh wind low. I open the cage door. *He* remains.

Fox blood is sour, *His* small head wounded.

I am afraid of *His* teeth, *His* grim-shine eyes. Mostly I am afraid of *His* voice

He could kill me with *His* stories. *He* could kill my baby.

I bludgeoned my wife, *He* tells me. I broke the blood of her flesh. I broke the thin bones of her fingers for touching another man.

I branded her ribs with fists.

I stabbed her with a fire stick blazing to sear her to me. She turned so many colors the Sky could no longer please me.

Who is she? I ask.

Wife for Dark Nights, *He* answers. Wife for Dark Nights Wife for Dark Nights   Wife for Dark Nights   Wife for Dark Nights Wife for Dark Nights.

I am sick with grief. I pray for what cannot be. I pray *Fox* takes pity on these white men who cause so much trouble. I pray *Fox* takes pity on Many Teeth.

I pray *Fox* takes pity on me and my baby.

Days of York talks

I know you understand what I'm saying to you. I got eyes to see.

You see this craziness here? I got to get it across to you how crazy these white bastards are—they got nothing. What they got is guns to kill. What they got is their small white dicks fucking everyone and everything.

The porcupine quills on your moccasins, the baskets you make, the matts you weave, the knowings you have—don't you see? That's worth something. If you ever been to their cities you'd see big buildings on top of buildings, the puss of them rising from their festering souls. They live in boxes on top of each other and spread their diseases.

Now they're trampling this beautiful country.

Makes me sick. I get sick every time I think about it. Because what they want is every goddamn thing! They ain't lookin' to discover nothin'. The reason these people are white is they already dead.

I long for my wife. I think of her every minute, every day. I gotta get home. I gotta get back to my Woman. They got her believing in the white man's bible. She says, Jesus will save us. At least Lewis and Clark don't believe that horseshit. I'll give them that. But the white men in their white cities, saying they love their god so much. So goddamn much! Sweet Jesus, they say all the time. Sweet Jesus they love their god so much that he becomes one of them. And then, they hate him so much because he's become one of them that they kill him. I do not lie. And then Jesus loves them back so much he dies to save them from their hateful selves.

There's something wrong with you when you need a god to love you for what you hate in yourself.

I see you Indians fighting over this and fighting over that and the whole while these devils are tracking you. Following you with their measures and surveys.

I'll tell you one thing I can't tell another soul. These white men come with me when I enter Indian Lodges. I never fucked one Indian without their eyes on me. I don't mean their flesh and blood eyes. I mean their spirit eyes. They were in there with me the whole time I was fucking those women.

White men spook me. Killing is their fucking. But I'd fuck every woman from here to home if I could spend one moment with my wife. I'd pray to Jesus if I could live with her. Lord, I miss her. Lord, how I miss her.

Days of Pomp

Baby giggles. Baby jigs. A taunt Fish.

I stop to tether his feet. Pomp kicks free. I feel his Eagle peck, his Rabbit thump, his Fox kick to my back.

We climb steep banks up and up. The weight of baby pulls me backward. I feel the tip at the top of my spine, the tumble dust I follow. Someone presses his hand to my shoulder and pushes me forward.

A Horse! A Horse! Lewis says, My kingdom for a Horse!

In the middle of men, baby and me. Whip wind. Heat slavers my back.

I push forward. Day spills with sweat.

Pomp shits like Bear. Leak all down me. His green dribble scorches.

Men gag.

Flies swirl round. We go on and on to the place where the Dead gather.

Warning days

Wind blows and blows and boats swirl. We travel where World stops and Water laps over us.

When wind stops, Moppo cloud the boats. Men slap themselves. Cover themselves in calamine.

I burn damp grasses until thick smoke clouds me.

Day of desecration

We climb through thick woods where Smudge lingers.
must-not-be-named is All Around.

I do not gather berries or seed grasses here. I do not strip chew bark. Men trample Burial ground without looking.

Charbonneau pushes me forward and I dodge him. Every time he reaches for me, I duck him.

It's uneasy here, Sergeant Ordway says. Even he sniffs the twittering sting of rot flesh and bone. Glug .. glug .. glug glug .. he swallows.

Lewis's dog paws what he should not paw. He drools over Burials. Seaman digs, until Lewis tethers him.

I see what they gawk at. A Burial scaffold of a Woman. Her Burial robe has split. I see the mouse-scatter cage of her ribs. Roots twist long fingers through her body. A dog rests beside her, mouth rotted into forever snarl.

The men stand in circle of no wind. A cocoon of quiet. Beyond their circle Trees flail. Trees rustle. Trees moan and creak. Branches snap and snap like someone walks around us.

I step far back from these men and return to Cruzatte and York. I wish to be far from the defilers. I cover Pomp's head. I cover my eyes.

Charbonneau bounds after me and snatches at me until he snares my arm.

When Clark cannot hear me, Charbonneau yanks Pomp from me and clatters him down to hard ground. Jean Baptiste is so stunned he does not cry. I reach for him but Charbonneau holds my hands and twists until my skin bubbles. He grabs my neck scruff and walks me to where they are looking, where they are poking, where they are desecrating.

I turn to see Cruzatte lift Pomp.

I will not look. I will not par-ti-ci-pate. I keep my eyes down. *Spirit* winks from thatch grass. Death shudders, quakes.

I thank Earth for my Life. I pray for Women, and the Woman they prod, for her dog, for her long journey.

Clark scribbles and scribbles and later will make us listen to his writings for today. He has cataloged Death that cannot be cataloged.

The night is so dark Lewis burns torches.

Clark curses us with a reading of his deed.

the wind became hard and waves so rough that we proceeded with our little canoes with much risqué, our situation was such after setting out that we were obliged to pass round the 1st Point or lay exposed to the blustering winds & waves, in passing round the Point several canoes took in water as also our large Perogue but without injuring our stores &c. much   a short distance below our Camp I saw some rafts on the S.S. near which, an Indian woman was scaffeled in the Indian for of Deposing their Dead and fallen down   She was or had been raised about 6 feet, inclosed in Several robes tightly laced around her, with her dog Slays, her bag of Different coloured earths paint small bones of animals beaver nales and Several trinkets, also a blue jay, her dog was killed and lay near her.

I try not to hear. They do not know the weight the Dead carry. How they carry *Her* weight now. How their poke and prod has opened us to the weight of all Dead.

Far far into on when my hands fail and my seeing withers, this day will bring shame.

Night of what is lost returns

No one sleeps. Fire pops and smokes.

I sit closer to Clark.

Light fl-flickers through woods. Here .. There.

Not Coyote yips, ... dog growls. Not bats, ... Blue Jays zitter overhead.

A Star sears Sky.

Pomp cries and cries. Whine-cry—blubber-cry—scared-cry.

Clark sings so low his voice carries through Trees.

In Scarlet town where I was born,

There was a fair maid dwellin'

Foul smell of mud-yellow rock steams up from the deep scent of Burial mounds. *Spirit Woman* thrums. Snaggle grass. Marsh weed glitter. Wrapped in tule and dry Antelope skin *She*

crack .. cracks .. cracks .. crack-s-s .. as *She* steps .. toward us.

Made every youth cry Well-a-day,

Her name was Barb'ra Allen.

Glug Glug stacks more wood on the fire. Glug Glug blinks blinks.

What comes is not good.

She returns as white as Fish scales. In the red fire roar, *Her* face. *Many Teeth.*

She circles the food cache, the tents of not one sleeping. We hear *Her* whoosh-swirl like the glug-snivel of Moose drinking Water as *She* slips beneath grasses and then slips beside us.

The big black dog paws Lewis, rootles beneath his robe.

Glug Glug's eyes wobble round. York looks at *Her* then looks away. His teeth ch-chatter.

Do not say *Her* name, I whisper to Jean Baptiste. *She* is Death. And more than we know. In Death *She* follows us. If you say *Her* name *She* will always follow us.

If Lewis or Clark would look up from their maps, would look up from picking the crusty blisters on their feet, they might see *Her*. Wife for Dark Nights sits between them unable to choose which white man will save *Her*.

Appe says, After bad Death a *crazy Spirit* rises.

Wife for Dark Nights howls in *Her crazy Spirit*. *She* laughs when we laugh. *She* laughs so hard snow rumbles from Mountains, laughs so hard River splutters, so hard *Her* laughter daggers us.

White men's eyes are blind as dim ice, blind as the yolk egg of quails.

Meriwether says, It's cold tonight, don't you think? There's a chill.

They do not know Wife for Dark Nights elbows between them. They do not see *Her*, breath, stilled, how *She* moves beside them, over them, Death. They do not see how they left *Her* with a Husband who stabbed *Her* to Death because white men did not want *Her* after they defiled *Her*. White men left *Her* behind like all the carcasses they judge, the pelts they weigh and catalog, the things they discard. All they see is plenty. With so much plenty, with so much Fish and Beaver, Buffalo and Women, nothing matters but choice. Their choice.

Wife for Dark Nights does not know they left *Her* behind at Mandan. She has forgotten stumbling to our campfire, shivering with fear. *She* has forgotten dying when we left her behind.

Only morning light shifts to touch Wife for Dark Nights; day sprays through the knife slits of *Her* ribs.

The River of the Dead follow us

They run ahead and beside us. They hang from Trees, spooky as black moss. A crazy Warrior follows York. His thin blade snipes air, whooshes York's heartbeat blood.

The *mean Spirit* of Lost His Head to Horse finds me again. He climbs on top of me when I bathe, when I shit, when I sleep. But I am not afraid. He has no power. His rape is puny, less than a Horse fly bite, a hornet sting. I have been plundered. I give him no more me.

River is dense with all the bodies white men leave in the wake of their canoes. Their big boats, their swivel guns blunting forward, up River veins, up Mountains, up Gather paths, up Women cunts.

So many Dead. So many gone. All the now Dead and all the Dead to be, stark-eyed as Crows they stare at the blind white men. Only Black Man can see them, and only rarely, when the Moon threads the needles of high Trees, when the grasses thread the hard soles of his boots.

York is sad and sick and drinks and dances.

Day ..

They go on into Mountains and Prairies and Canyons and Valleys. They cross and defile Rivers where Agai fight to live. They slog sandy Streams and piss where animals drink and rest. They enter what they should not enter and name what *must-not-be-named*.

If we name all things, we kill the gifts they offer.

Clark speaks of great cities where stone Lodges are taller than the tallest Tree, where men can shut out People with heavy doors made of gun metal. But here the Land is open to them. Free.

How can they go to places where they do not belong? Guns give War men entry. They talk about their weapons like Women: Pennsylvania-style, single shot muzzle-loading flintlock rifles, blunderbuss, cannon swivel, contract rifles, squirrel guns, Clark's gentleman gun, Horseman's pistols.

And they kill Bears just for the killing. And now ..

Everywhere Bear tracks. Every day men shoot Bears but the great Bears come back. At night, Bears squat All Around, their eyes black and round and bigger than musket balls.

White men count the bullets they fire into Bear. Their heavy bullets sear both Bear lungs. A bullet to the shoulder. A bullet to his haunches. Bear changes gait and keeps on charging. No amount of gunpowder startles Bear. No amount of bullets. Round balls pelt, pierce, bludgeon Bears—two and then four, four and then six, six and then eight. Bear charges through the yellow-green haze of gunpowder blasts. Bear chase men into Rivers. Bear chase men off bluffs. Bear so furious they hunt men.

And Rattlesnakes!

Rattlesnakes longer than the height of a tall man coil on the banks, on the bluffs, everywhere.

We hear their buzzing.

Moppo and blackflies swirl and pelt. Great swarms of mosquitoes. Black clouds over men.

Why don't the bugs bother you? the white men ask.

Not a mosquito lands on me. Not a fly grazes me.

You must have some Injun medicine you're not sharing.

I do not smile. Too Ott Lok. Too Ott Lok gifts me.

I read sign of all creaking Trees, of all animals spying us, of Owls hoot voice, of Voles scrittering in caches, of Bird swoops and Eagle screeches and Fox paws and Coyote cries and camps abandoned. Great Water falls—*go away hiss.*

Wife for Dark Nights swims in the swirled Water, and when *She* rises, *She* spits Water at men but they believe *She* is only a sudden rush of wind, a large rock churning Water.

If they would look longer into white-lipped tongues of currents they might see *Her.*

Wife for Dark Nights twirls past the canoes.

All night *She* rides the muddy-Mooned Waters.

Days of give up

Lewis bleeds me with leeches. I am hot with fever. Sick.

I cannot feed Jean Baptiste.

York is sent to kill for milk.

I wake to Pomp sucking a sugar teat. I fall into sleep so deep I feel my heavy bone weight pulling me down.

I doubt she'll make it, Lewis says. We need her. If nothing more than a shield, a safeguard. A woman who appears to come in peace. And what of Pomp? Who will take care of him?

Clark promises his man will. Pomp will stay alive with York.

Lewis and Clark sit outside the tent, close to hear me breathing. They drink until their voices slur and become loud.

We could stuff her and put her at the helm of the boat, Lewis says. These Indians would never know.

That'd be good, Clark says. Good grief. That'd be one desperate solution. They sputter-laugh.

York sits beside me. Don't listen to those bastards, he whispers. Get well. You're almost home. Almost home. Almost home.

In York's voice, I hear Blue Elk's voice. Come to me, he says.

Have you been standing here since I left you? Old Woman asks.

I know not to stare but cannot keep my eyes away.

Now come, she tells me. The People need their Buffalo and all this time I've been talking.

We come out of the woods and emerge onto a bluff over Mandan Prairies. Old Woman steps to the rattlly edge and we look out over the wide Buffalo plain. We see far below and far into the distance.

Thunder rumbles. Sky zings purple and once-hidden Deer and Antelope turn orange, Lightning bright. They cannot hide.

As far as we can see, no Buffalo. Without Buffalo the Prairie is gutted.

Rain falls in silver robes.

Old Woman sits on a rock and begins her story.

A long time ago, the People were starving. Many Hunt parties went to find Buffalo and they returned empty-handed. The Buffalo had vanished.

We believed we had insulted Buffalo. Buffalo had given themselves and given of themselves and we had given nothing in return.

A young girl went on a journey to ask Buffalo to return. She traveled far to the great Lodges of Buffalo and called to them. She asked Buffalo to forgive the People. She left Tobacco and Corn.

She saw Buffalo dancing on the high Prairie. On and on Buffalo danced. She went to join them in the dance. She did not know it was Enemy disguised as Buffalo. She danced and danced with Enemy, and Buffalo, seeing the young girl dance, came out of their Lodges to join her.

More Buffalo came and more Buffalo. Earth roared with Buffalo running. Buffalo did not know Enemy tricked them. Soon a great herd had come, and still more Buffalo came. They charged into the dance, and the wind of their passing pulled them all over the Buffalo jump. Whole herds of Buffalo clattered down on the girl.

After Enemy had taken all the Buffalo they could take, the young girl was left behind, buried beneath Buffalo. Her poor body twisted and broken. She was so disfigured Buffalo took pity on her. They took her back to their Lodges. They healed her. They called her Sister.

Buffalo told her from this day on she would never be harmed. They promised whenever she called, Buffalo would return to the People.

I will take you back now, Old Woman says, but you will have to fight to return.

Her mirrors flicker. Do you know Weta follows you? she asks. They've been trying to kill her but they cannot.

But they did kill her. They killed many Bears.

Onion Wife called Weta, Old Woman tells me. Did you not know?

Onion Wife called *must-not-be-named* for White Crow, I tell her. She called *what-should-not-have-been-called*.

Old Woman nods her head as she looks at me. Stories are not always remembered the way they happened, she says.

Old Woman's mirrors begin to glitter, to twitch with stories, to shine with voices.

Do not trust anyone who tells you you cannot tell your story.

Do not trust anyone who tells you there is only one story.

If there were only one story

Or one way of seeing things all stories would die.

The winter of White Crow's Death ..

Blood did not scab
Mouths became as blue as distant hills—
Breast milk became sour water
Babies curled inward seeking marrow heat. Heart heat.
Your Babies became as brittle as
yellow leaves
as light as Milkweed ..

Stink wind rose up from the bog cold. Up from the spiked weeds
of frozen marshes with the odorous breath
of *Weta*
who had eaten

Death.
Weta's rotten plop berries. Weta's oily shit.
Her scat pebbled snow.
Wind rattled Lodges and snaked away fire heat. Cold chased up
sleep robes
burned white circles on Men's faces
.. blackened .. their fingers .. stank.
Your People believed this *Weta* was a curse sent by your great Enemy
the Apsáalooke
for poisoning their War party.
The People were wrong.
The great stinging heart of sorrow called *Weta*.
Onion Wife's grief called *Weta*.
The People could feel before they saw
Hear before they understood
poison ponds, hair tugs, snag hooks, all things
SPIT from the lungs of her vengeance.

Clacking bones .. *Clacking* bones .. *Clacking* bones .. *Clacking*
bones ..
Her
Furious Breath
Called up *Weta* made of
.. shatter bones .. breast bones .. thigh bones .. broke
knuckle bones ..
Her
Feverish Breath
Called up
Slivers of their teeth their ribs their hips their elbows
Her
Fuming Breath
Called up

eyes not eyes .. placenta black gut from the sluice of Women bodies.

Her
Ferocious Breath
called
Weta in her bone robe of Women suffer to stalk Men who
defile Women.

Can you hear *Weta* clicking with the bones of Women suffer?
She is circling.

Weta, her coat the color of Moon lit up, snatched *men* from the
field where they hid after bludgeoning, after raping, after defiling
White Crow
color of bone
color of hunger
color of blood spit and gristle
As *Weta* moved closer your People heard the cries of Women

                    calling from
                          the cage of
                          Weta's ribs.

Your People hear your cries and wait for your return, Old
Woman tells me. She reaches for me but cannot touch.
    Onion Wife called *must-not-be-named* for you, my Daughter.
Me? I ask.

I know now. To wake to All Around means my story will
change me from now into on. I have been all along dreaming.

RETURN

Day of Horses

We come to cliffs where Rattlers dwell. Rattlers tick in the belly Canyon and when Clark tosses rocks, furious Rattlers shake above, around us.

Charbonneau holds on to me.

I sign to Clark this is a place I have been before. We are not far from my People.

He tells the others we are on the right path, but the men are hesitant. They Fish mouth and scuttle. They do not wish to climb steep cliffs where Rattlers sun on ledges. They sneer.

At the base of the cliffs, Earth is soft. Snake trails wortle round boulders and rocks. Musky scent of plum rises from rocks close to where we walk, and the men ah and oodle and say it smells like cucumbers. They do not know it is the smell of riled snakes.

Lewis fires and the spear head flops on a flat rock where its huge jaws open and close. The fat snake twists and waggles in the soft dirt. Men laugh. Even dead, Rattlers bite, they say.

I sit by the fire until Moon becomes thin as a sliver. Men shift, snore, and talk to each other in sleep. Two Brothers call out to their Bia as if they are together in sleep, as if the day goes on for them.

Another sleepwalks. He stands at the tent flap and chatters. His oily eyes plead, his voice rises and sputters, and a shimmery light comes. I am sorry, Sergeant Floyd, he says. I am sorry.

Baptiste sleeps at my breast, his heat unbearable to me. Having to carry, having to suckle with sore teats, having to feed, to clothe him. I will rest soon.

My journey with white men ends tomorrow. Charbonneau will be gone. I will be rid of him.

Blue Elk sleeps a night ride away. He is so close he is my breath.

I have walked these fields. I have smelled these grasses. These Trees. I am close to all I ache for, close to all my Relations. I cannot sleep.

Day of the long walk

Because I know every step, every step grows longer as I walk. Just over this hill. Just beyond that rise. Past this Tree. That bush. I stop to feed Jean Baptiste and he is ruckus and leap. He toddles on wobbly legs away from me. I do not have to chase him. No white man will dust him. No animal will snag him.

Lewis left the day before.

Charbonneau puddle foots behind. Slow. I bounce like Deer. I loop back. I catch Charbonneau up and he blows his lips at me.

When I smell River scent and Sweetgrass my legs wobble like Jean Baptiste's legs. No place smells like this place. I stop and breathe. I flop down and rub my hands in Earth. I want to roll like a cub.

Someone in the distance rides toward us .. Men .. .. My People. I run toward them and stop to run back to Charbonneau. Why do I run to you? I ask. I speak my language and he grimaces. I hold my head and spin.

Charbonneau takes Jean Baptiste. He signs for me to calm. You are making a fuss, Charbonneau tells me in Hidatsa. Calm down. But over in the distance I see a spark of light.

I cannot catch my breath. I hold my side ache.

When I see Clark, I laugh, and he laughs with me. Many People are coming toward me. They surround me and embrace me. Onion Wife makes her way to me and holds my hands so tightly I see Bia. The People, my People, turn to someone coming toward me. I see the top of her head before I see her.

She struggles to get to me.

.. I look .. I cannot believe .. I cannot believe .. I bite my fingers ..

Li-li-li-li, I shout. Women join me. Li-li-li-li-li-li, we call.

I cannot hold what overflows me. I am River.

Earth is berries and River sounds. She returns for me from Death. From capture. From Womb hurt. From killing winter River.

Pop Pank, Pop Pank, Pop Pank, Pop Pank.

I gather her like beloved Earth.

A Sister alive.

A Sister returned.

Women surround me. They bring me robes and dried Agai. They jiggle and pass Jean Baptiste. They gossip.

Bawitčhuwa is with Blue Elk, they tell me. She has not had any babies. He wants to see you but she does not want him to come near you. She is still stingy.

I seek Combs Gut and tell her Too Ott Lok lives among the Many Spirit People at Mandan. She listens quietly. She listens with her gut. He is wise and kind now, not plagued by Moppo. His name is Walks Many Ways, I tell her.

Combs Gut kisses my hands. My Too Ott Lok, she says. My Too Ott Lok.

I tell Onion Wife that Running Woman is a Sister to the Mandan. I tell her she sings in the high Corn fields. No one can match her, I say.

I stumble in my telling. She can outrun any man, I say. She is a great and honored Storyteller.

Yes, Onion Wife says, that is the story that must go on.

They ask why I live with white man, and before I answer, I am called to Cameahwait's Lodge.

Lewis and Clark want Shoshoni Horses. They gadder among themselves. In front of me and my Brother, the Chief, they talk as if we are trade goods. Do they think we do not understand? They say we are fickle and childish People.

Do they not know I have traveled with them a long way? I have slept in their Lodges. I have fed them, walked beside them, heard them speak every day. Even Magpies know what we say. Crows speak many tongues. I would be a fool not to hear their language.

Lewis and Clark ask me through Charbonneau to tell Cameahwait they have a plan to pay for Horses, but I tell my brother they are pitiful men who need help. I feel safe to say what I think.

Days of Blue Elk

Blue Elk finds me and Bawitčhuwa chases after. She grabs his hand. She tugs. She clutches his arm when he comes close to me.

Blue Elk's hair is shining and silvering. Bawitčhuwa is round and full and pregnant with living, although she has no children.

I cannot stop looking. Blue Elk is beautiful. Bawitčhuwa is beautiful. Together they scent me with River grasses, plait me with sweet root.

River Ogres peer from their rock caves. River silvers beneath Debai. Cottonwood Trees flutter.

Mud Squatter.

Appe.

Here my Bia taught me to cache seeds. Here Bia taught me.

I call to the self I cannot collect. The place that is me and not me.

I hear |He is woman| talk about oceans. The salt of it. The blue, the gray, the white, the wind of sea. So much Water you cannot swim to the bottom. Ocean waves roar and fizz and pull you out if you are not watchful. So much Water holds other Worlds. *Spirit Worlds of Water.* And Whales. Whales are Fish so big you could live inside them.

Clark brings Jean Baptiste to me. Charbonneau squeezes my arm and pulls me to him.

This is my Son, I say. I hold Jean Baptiste up. Jean Baptiste wiggles and drools. When I put him down he runs from me again. When did he become so fast?

Charbonneau rests his chin on my shoulder. When I do not look at him, he stands tall and places his hand on my neck, and I fear he will grab me by the ruff.

Is he this white man's child? Blue Elk asks.

He is my child, I say.

He is your child by a white man.

I do not answer. Blue Elk turns from me. I follow.

I have come back to you, I say. I have traveled far, over Mountains, across Valleys and Rivers. I have been beaten. I have been tatter broken and starved. I have worked my way back to you. Why did you not come for me?

I will not be with a Woman who has had a white man's child, he says.

Only Bawitčhuwa answers with a tongue cluck. She places her hand on her Husband and they turn from me.

Even with Cameahwait I cannot stop crying. I feel shame.

Pop Pank gathers me. I do not cover my face. I stand.

Lewis looks my way. I hope we can get Horses, he says. This is trouble. I had no idea, he says. She's never shown one wit of emotion. Her outburst is surprising.

Clark glances at me. He lifts Pomp in his arm and holds him tight.

Jesus, Lewis, he says. She was stolen from these people. The man she lives with beats her.

I need to settle up with Charbonneau so I can get custody of Pomp.

I don't understand, Lewis says. But yes, yes. Do what you must. He's lucky to have you.

at day's end

Dusk returns to River. Sky is turning.

My Relations celebrate. They thrill to York. I hear their laughter.

I am rain in dry skies that will not be returning.

Someone comes. I burrow down on myself.

Puh, Bia says. Why you cry for man who lives with nothing-good-woman?

I turn to No-one-is-there.

Three Forks.

Light shines on all Rivers. Pink light, the color of a baby foot. I put my feet in River and Water cools like camphor.

There you are, Clark calls. Someone has been looking for you.

Jean Baptiste jumps at me. Clark has to grab him.

Hold on sweet Pomp, he says.

Jean Baptiste stretches his arms out to me, and when I hold him, he knocks his big head to my chest .. Thump .. Thump .. Thump .. My Jack Rabbit. My boy. He opens his mouth and I feel his drooly tongue on my chin. He fists my hair and chews. He whimpers.

He is heavy in my arms. Bia, he says. Bia. Bia.

I hold him in my arms. I sleep in my Brother's Lodge. I dream of Agai. I dream of Whales.

Day of good Water

York smiles when he sees me mounted on Horse with Jean Baptiste on my lap.

When Lewis sees me, I hold my legs tight. I am a suck bug. They will not remove me. I am going. I am going to the sea. I will see the Whales. I have traveled all this way. If I have to tell them in English, I will tell them, I go with them. They cannot stop me.

Lewis turns to Clark, Good grief, he says.

I knew, York whispers, you're a Woman who survives.

Debai winks through Cottonwoods and lights River.

Bawitčhuwa comes to watch me leave. She strikes me with her look:

I wish her all good days into on.

I wish her children, up ahead, where she goes on to better.

I wish her always Blue Elk. I wish her long days with our People. But even more—

I wish her the jittery Stars that will always lead her home.

In the crackle grasses, Weta runs beside us.

A leafy flap flutters

Come in, she tells me.

There is something I must show you.

Her dwelling is as small as a Woman's blood hut. Bladder smell, childbirth, bone-snap-strike, pain.

Mice scritter, lick, gnaw. Bats swoop and twirl overhead and I smell the dull scent of their oil-sleek wings, hear the shriek of their tiny voices squeezed through needle throats, and Birds, the drum drum of hag Crows, the beating wing roar of ten thousand Hummingbirds. Blunt noses of Eagles poke Her grass roof, screeching. Rut blood. Women's blood.

Old Woman is a nesty coil of silver meat peels, egg shatter, lance boil, knife-edge blood, urine soak, brain hide.

She was old before; now She is ancient.

She sits coiled in on Herself, around, around, a round Earth lump, a Rattler sweet as piss and Women cunt. And old, so old Her bones loop down and down like ancient woven grass rope breaking. Plump and round and plum dark. Her skin worn in places like grass matts. Her eyes the color of Rabbit gut, white pink.

When She moves, the caldron of Her ribs hiss.

Walk with me, Daughter, She says.

We walk through forests lit with Bluebirds. Hawks wing overhead. Deer follow. She leads me to a great precipice and I see the vast Waters. A great Whale butchered. I smell salt and Death and bones. I smell molder. I see white Birds flying over the great blue Waters and the light is so bright it burns. My eyes Stream.

Her mirror light blinds me.

Look again, She says. Tell me what you see.

I squint to see the Land of my Appe and Bia, my People, Agaidika, more beautiful than all the People. I see the deep, scented Waters of Agai River, and red Agai struggling up River to spawn. I see berries and seeds and root Land. Trees and mint and Mountain Streams. I see River Ogres and hear crying Water Babies. I see *Mud Squatter's River Spirit* now turned the color of River rocks, waiting.

I see jangle-boom flood Waters covering Metaharta. The People crying.

In the glittering dark mirror, I see nümü pahamittsi hiding.

I see the vast Prairie. Grasses withering to white man weeds.

I see a crooked girl, body broken at the waist and twisted back on herself. Crooked girl walks forward but faces backward. She is crickety in her walk. She moves like an animal shot and left to die. She struggles in her walk. She toils. Buffalo nudge her. Buffalo run beside her, around her. Buffalo calves lick her broken hands, her splinter-broken feet.

The young girl lifts her arms to Sky and I feel the great Earth shake. I see the split Sky, a blue vein above, an ocean of kicked dirt below.

Far

far

in the distance

I see Buffalo full charge—a rampage of Buffalo—as if all the Buffalo herds of all the Buffalo Nations joined together.

Buffalo come because the young girl calls them. They come because she is one with them. Their bones clattered and splintered together as they fell over the Buffalo jump. When we suffer together our bones knit as one. In the rising dust she dances, and her dance calls the People together. She Walks with Buffalo.

To Walk with Buffalo is to bring what is Dead back to living.

When the Buffalo are gone, the Prairie will die, Old Woman says.

You are the last traditional Woman to see the great Buffalo herds. You prayed over the last path of the Buffalo.

Who are you? I ask.

I am Woman Who Has Always Lived, she tells me. Do you see?

I see hazed red Debai, great cauldrons of Buffalo dust, smoke from thousands and thousands of rifles. Buffalo blood like flooding Waters. Stacks of bones. Mountains of dead Buffalo rotting. I see bones, more bones—a great white fire rising over the vast Land they roamed.

I see myself.

ACKNOWLEDGMENTS

Thank you, Laura Millin and Steve Glueckert, who first convinced me I should tackle Lewis & Clark in service of the Missoula Art Museum (MAM).

Thank you, Peter Koch, who gave vision to the original version of this story.

Thank you, Susan Filter, for your foresight to insist on this story.

Thank you, Rich Wandschneider and the good people of the The Josephy Center for Arts and Culture (JCAC), who have enriched the lives of many.

Thank you, Nancy Knoble, for your gracious hospitality in the last leg of this story.

Thank you, Whitney Williams, for your friendship and immeasurable support.

Thank you, Johnny Arlee, for remembering old stories of astounding possibilities not found in any history books.

Thank you, Guggenheim Foundation. Your support not only changed my life, it affirmed my life's path.

Thank you, Centrum, for offering me refuge to write.

Thank you, Sally Wofford-Girand. You're fierce and brilliant! You've believed in me throughout the long journey.

Thank you, Marianna Di Paolo, Director of WRMC Shoshoni Language Project & Center for American Indian Languages, for so kindly answering my email.

Thank you, Daniel Slager and Broc Rossell. Thank you, Lauren Langston Klein, for brilliantly carrying the story to completion. No one could ask for more attentive and spirit-boosting editors. Thank you, Mary Austin Speaker, for your visionary art. Thank you, Kachina Yeager and Yanna Demkiewicz. Thank you, Milkweed Editions.

Thank you to my wonderful friends who listened and believed: Annick Smith, Adrianne Harun, Melissa Kwasny, Lisa Simon, Mandy Smoker, Lynn-Wood Fields, Pat Williams, Kerry Dolan, Chris Dombrowski, Sheila Black, Caroline Patterson, Kevin Head, Colleen O'Brien, Brenna Reitman, Deborah Hern, Tracy Cosgrove, Tim Gordon, Rita Pyrillis, Vicki Chaney, Chip Livingston, Stephanie Wing, Kelley Willett, Sho Campbell, Dixie Reynolds, Georgia Porter, Vonda Stubblefield, and always for my brother Dennis, and Gayle.

Robert Stubblefield, thank you for always making it easy.

DEBRA MAGPIE EARLING is the author of *The Lost Journals of Sacajewea* and *Perma Red*. She has received a National Endowment for the Arts grant, a Guggenheim Fellowship, and the Montana Book Award. She retired from the University of Montana where she was named professor emeritus in 2021. She is Bitterroot Salish.

milkweed
EDITIONS

Founded as a nonprofit organization in 1980, Milkweed Editions is an independent publisher. Our mission is to identify, nurture, and publish transformative literature, and to build an engaged community around it.

Milkweed Editions is based in Bdé Óta Othúŋwe (Minneapolis) within Mní Sota Makhóčhe, the traditional homeland of the Dakhóta people. Residing here since time immemorial, Dakhóta people still call Mní Sota Makhóčhe home, with four federally recognized Dakhóta nations and many more Dakhóta people residing in what is now the state of Minnesota. Due to continued legacies of colonization, genocide, and forced removal, generations of Dakhóta people remain disenfranchised from their traditional homeland. Presently, Mní Sota Makhóčhe has become a refuge and home for many Indigenous nations and peoples, including seven federally recognized Ojibwe nations. We humbly encourage our readers to reflect upon the historical legacies held in the lands they occupy.

milkweed.org

Milkweed Editions, an independent nonprofit literary publisher, gratefully acknowledges sustaining support from our board of directors, the McKnight Foundation, the National Endowment for the Arts, and many generous contributions from foundations, corporations, and thousands of individuals—our readers. This activity is made possible by the voters of Minnesota through a Minnesota State Arts Board Operating Support grant, thanks to a legislative appropriation from the arts and cultural heritage fund.